She was assailed by uneasy doubts

Dawn willingly agreed to locate an old friend for her brother. It seemed a simple task until she learned he'd died – how, no one would reveal. His widow, Alys, especially resented her inquiries....

Her alarm grew when she met an artist who warned her against Alys. He refused to say why, except that his brother had married Alys...and now he was dead. Uneasy, Dawn sensed he was deliberately withholding the truth. But why?

One thing was certain: either someone was lying to her – or someone was playing a deadly game.

Other

MYSTIQUE BOOKS

by MAGALI

For a free catalogue listing all available Mystique Books,
send your name and address to:

MYSTIQUE BOOKS
M.P.O. Box 707, Niagara Falls, NY 14302
In Canada: 649 Ontario St., Stratford, Ontario N5A 6W2

Love in Jeopardy

by MAGALI

MYSTIQUE BOOKS
TORONTO • LONDON • NEW YORK
HAMBURG • AMSTERDAM • STOCKHOLM

LOVE IN JEOPARDY / first published February 1981

ISBN 0-373-50113-7

Chapter 1

"You're sure this is the right place?" I asked the cab driver, staring in distaste at a large canvas heavily daubed with violent-colored oils. Admittedly, I knew nothing about abstract art, but I did know what I liked, and this wasn't it. In fact, I was surprised to see it in the gallery window, for I didn't think it was Maurice's taste in art, either.

"This is the address you gave me," replied the driver, rather huffily.

I glanced up at the brass numbers nailed above the door and had to acknowledge the truth of this statement. Then my eye traveled downward, and to my disappointment I saw that the door was locked and bolted. Very obviously the gallery was closed.

"You can always check with the concierge," suggested the driver, and with a squeal of tires drove off before I had a chance to stop him.

The concierge, I thought, *that most venerable of Parisian institutions; those building superintendents who collectively always seem to know everything that goes on in the city. I wonder how often they come to the rescue of visitors in trouble?*

The concierge of this particular building turned out to

be an old woman, whom I found in a gloomy little office at the end of a darkened hallway. The office was lit by a single, naked bulb hanging down the center of a grimy ceiling and throwing harsh shadows on the equally grimy walls. As I looked around at the indescribable clutter in this dingy little room it seemed as if all the brilliant sunshine outside, all the cheery delight of springtime in Paris, had suddenly disappeared.

I stopped on the threshold, hesitant to enter, but the old woman waved me inside. "Can I help you?" she asked, in a seemingly friendly tone.

"My name is Dawn Charbonneau," I told her. "I'm looking for Maurice Briançon."

"You want to buy some pictures?"

I thought of the painting I'd seen in the window and barely suppressed a shudder. "No," I replied. "I just want to meet with him."

"I'm afraid it's impossible. He isn't here."

"I noticed the gallery was closed. Can you tell me when he'll be back?"

The old woman shrugged. "Never," she replied.

"But . . . but isn't this his art gallery?" I stammered, taken aback by this unexpected reply.

"It *was*," she corrected, "but he sold the business some time ago. He's been gone for months."

For a moment I simply stared at her in dismay. Having arrived in Paris early that morning, after a long and arduous trip from Canada, I'd spent most of the day so far looking for my brother's old friend from his university days.

Norman had met Maurice Briançon twenty years earlier when he'd been a student at the Sorbonne, the oldest and most famous university in France. During his infrequent trips home, my brother would amuse me with epic accounts of all the wild times the two of them had living it up in Paris, between bouts of studying.

Norman had shared a room with Maurice, who, like

him, was taking courses at the Sorbonne. They both had very happy memories of that time they'd shared together, but having completed their arts degrees, had had to think seriously about making a living, and went their separate ways. I was a little girl when Maurice came to spend two months with us one summer, shortly after Norman came home from France, but I could still see him clearly in my mind's eye—a tall, well-built, sturdy young man. I remembered how he used to burst into gales of laughter as he roughhoused with Eric, my younger brother. Maurice's behavior had shocked me at the time, but had also inspired in me a certain respect.

Maurice hadn't returned to visit us since, but we always spoke of him at Christmas time, when greeting cards were exchanged.

Eventually my brother had married and had children, and our lives drifted apart. I was busy with my own studies and with trying to make my way in the world. I heard nothing more about Maurice until the eve of my departure for Europe, when Norman and his wife came to say goodbye to me.

"Well, Dawn, I'm glad you're taking off for France," he said. "While you're there, I'd like you to do me a favor and look up my old friend Maurice." He chuckled, then continued in a tone of affectionate reproach, "That old so-and-so! For years he never answered my letters, never even gave any signs of life, in fact. Then, last year, he wrote me an urgent message, saying that he was planning to come to Canada, and asking me if I could put him up at my place for a while. He needed my help and advice on a problem he had."

Unfortunately this call for help had arrived while Norman was away. My brother—who has a lot of talent, and has incidentally made quite a name for himself as an interior designer—had gone off to decorate the ranch of a rich American in Arizona. His wife went with him and his secretary, thinking that Maurice's letter wasn't very important, hadn't bothered to forward it. After my brother had finished the job in Arizona, he'd taken a prolonged vacation in Bermuda with the family before returning home to Montreal.

"When I finally got back and found the letter," Norman explained, "some months had gone by. I immediately sent off a telegram to Maurice and followed it up with a letter, but I never received a reply. I wrote him again several times, but there was no response. And at Christmas, he didn't even reply to my greeting card. His silence really bothers me. Maybe he's annoyed at what he takes to be negligence on my part. I'm really very upset about this, so much so that, if you weren't going to France, I'd think of hopping on a plane and looking up the old rogue myself. He certainly seemed to be in trouble. But now it's up to you to rekindle our old friendship."

"Any idea what his problem was?" I asked.

"He gave me a couple of hints, but—" my brother wagged an admonishing finger in what I knew was a teasing gesture "—his private life is none of your business." Then he gave me an affectionate hug. "Just be a good little sister and find him for me, will you?"

I was quite willing to help Norman out. After all, I didn't know anyone in France, and no doubt Maurice could give me a few pointers on the Parisian life-style. He might be particularly helpful, I thought, in assisting me to find an apartment—a tough job, I knew.

Consequently, as soon as I'd checked into my hotel and freshened up somewhat from the trip, I'd set out in search of my brother's old friend. I started at his club, which was the last address he'd given Norman for letters to reach him, but was told he hadn't been seen there for some months. Why, asked the secretary, didn't I try his art gallery, located on rue Jacob?

Having discovered that the street in question was right

across the other side of Paris, I'd hired a taxi and done as she'd suggested, only to be confronted by this old woman with her disappointing news. Altogether, it had been a tiring and thoroughly frustrating morning.

"Well, can you tell me where he's living now?" I said weakly. Already I felt exhausted at the mere thought of dashing off to some other part of this vast and bustling city.

"Where he *was* living, you mean. He used to have an apartment out in the suburbs, at Versailles, but he's not there anymore."

"Just my luck!" I remarked bitterly.

At my obvious disappointment, the old woman suddenly became talkative, as if she felt an explanation of Maurice's disappearance could alleviate my frustration. "He came into some money," she explained. "One of his relatives died, I think, somewhere quite a ways from here, down south. I know he'd been over-worked and was feeling tired out and I remember he said to me one day, 'Mrs. Plante, I'm going home.'

"A week later he was gone. He'd already put the gallery up for sale long before and accepted the first offer that came along, from a strange fellow who doesn't seem to take much interest in running it at all. He just opens it from time to time when he feels like it. Why, just this morning some people came around to look at one of his paintings, the one in the window it was, but he was nowhere to be found. . . ."

The old woman's flow of gossip did not help my mood. "So, Mr. Briançon doesn't come here anymore?" I asked, hoping to cut it short.

But she ignored my question and mused, "I wonder how he managed to persuade his wife to leave Paris."

"His wife? He was married then?" I queried, suddenly realizing how little I really knew about Maurice Brian-çon. It had been quite a while since he'd broken off all correspondence with Norman, and I wondered if my brother had known he had a wife but had forgotten to tell me.

The concierge stared at me, sudden suspicion showing in her eyes. "You don't know Mr. Briançon's wife?" she asked, obviously not understanding how someone interested in his whereabouts could not know he was married.

"Well . . . no, I don't, actually" I replied, and to allay her suspicions, I made some effort to explain the relationship between Norman and Maurice.

"Well, that's all right then," she said, giving me a brief smile of relief when I'd finished. "I understand now why you're so interested in Mr. Briançon, and I think I can help you out. I'm sure I wrote down the name of his hometown somewhere."

She ferreted through the drawers of a grubby-looking little desk and emerged moments later waving a sheet of yellowed notepaper triumphantly. "Here's his address," she said. "You can keep it. I won't be needing it anymore."

Happy to have found some precise information at last, I thanked her and hurried out of the building, eager to get back into the sunshine and warmth of the street. I suddenly felt very hungry. Glancing at my watch, I realized that it was already two o'clock in the afternoon, and that all the running around that morning had sharpened my appetite.

I managed to find a typically Parisian bar-restaurant, a cozy little place where I ordered veal cutlets and mashed potatoes. While I was waiting for the waitress to set the table and bring my lunch, I took out the paper the concierge had given me and studied the address.

Maurice Briançon had moved back to his home in the Périgord. I remembered from my history and geography lessons in school that the Périgord was the name of one of the old provinces in France, down in the southwest part of the country near the great wine-growing district of Bordeaux, and that the region was still known by that name.

I realized that I'd have to make quite a lengthy and unexpected journey if I was going to convey my brother's apologies to his friend Maurice, but in a way, the prospect pleased me. Périgord, I knew, was a fascinating part of France, famous for its truffles and its pâté de foie gras, and for its magnificent prehistoric caves with their beautiful animal murals, of which the grottoes at Lascaux were the most widely known. Then, too, Périgord was a region rich in history, a center of civilization in the Middle ages and a rich prize that the kings of France and England had fought over for centuries. What better place to start my research?

I was in France for a year, courtesy of the Canadian Broadcasting Corporation. It hadn't been all that long ago, I realized, that I'd been just another fresh-faced trainee in the CBC's Montreal TV studios. But several years of hard work had paid off, and I'd moved up to become producer in my own right. Now the studio had granted me a year's sabbatical, partly to enable me to study French TV production methods, but mainly to give me time to scout around for good program ideas.

On my arrival in Paris that morning, I'd been hungry for impressions of this great capital that I'd so longed to see. And, indeed, to begin with, I had enjoyed the many new and varied sights and sounds. My taxi driver had pointed out some of the famous sights of Paris that I'd so often seen in prints and photographs. I, myself, had easily picked out Notre Dame Cathedral, the immense bulk of the Louvre Museum, Les Invalides where Napoleon was buried and the vast park of the Champ de Mars dominated by the Eiffel Tower.

As we drove along the riverside highway, I had gazed in fascination at the Seine, shimmering with pools of sunshine as it threaded its way under the great bridges of Paris. All along the river a host of barges and pleasure boats went on their cheery way, their pennants flapping jauntily in the breeze.

Well, I'd thought, *this really is the famous Paris, renowned in song and story.* I'd found myself enchanted by the spectacle of Place de la Concorde, with its many gushing fountains, and I had thought how pleasant it would be to stroll along the broad sidewalks of the Champs-Elysées, to savor its movie theaters, outdoor cafés, smart shops and store windows filled with luxury goods. Catching sight of the Arc de Triomphe, bathed in a soft spring light and framing a large piece of clear blue sky, I'd wanted to pause, to sit down at one of the elegant café terraces and drink in the magnificent vista.

However I hadn't had the time, and as the morning wore on and I dashed from one end of the city to the other in search of my brother's friend, I found myself feeling disappointed. In fact, as I'd gazed at the passing show of streets, congested almost beyond belief, I'd wanted nothing as much as peace and quiet and the wide-open spaces of the country I'd just left.

Now, sitting in yet another taxi, which I'd hired after lunch to take me back to my hotel, I felt the same desire to escape. I noticed the same store windows, the same boutiques, even the same modern furniture I'd already seen in other major cities around the world. As we reached the Arc de Triomphe, swung around it and headed down the Champs-Elysées, we immediately found ourselves surrounded by an astonishingly dense mass of vehicles and I had to make a conscious effort to appreciate the fact that I was now on one of the world's most beautiful thoroughfares. All I could see over the tops of the cars were the upper stories of the buildings on either side of the street. Where, I wondered, was the real Paris, and when would I begin to be aware of its secret wisdom, its profundities, and sense the ardor and the love that built it stone by stone over so many centuries. That was the Paris we children had dreamed of in the evenings of our long Canadian winters, when snowstorms shook the beech and maple trees that surrounded the wooden porch of our house, and we, cozy beside the fireplace, listened to our mother whisper stories of the greatness of old France.

No doubt, had I not been so tired and disoriented after my journey, I would have appreciated my first day in this country's great capital a little more. As it was, by the time I'd sent a brief telegram to Norman advising him of the situation concerning Maurice Briançon, I think I'd already made up my mind to go down to the Périgord in search of him, regardless of my brother's wishes on the subject. *I can always discover Paris later*, I thought, *little by little, one masterpiece at a time, the way a gourmet slowly savors an exquisite dish he's fancied for a long time.*

The day I spent waiting for Norman's reply merely firmed my resolve to leave the delights of Paris until later. I'd originally intended to travel after spending at least a month in Paris, but there was no reason I couldn't change my plan. I felt hemmed in by the city, threatened by claustrophobia, and I had an overwhelming need for greenery and fresh air.

My imagination began to fill with images of the Périgord—wooded landscapes, still waters and medieval fortresses. Apart from those gourmet delights that had given the area a reputation as an epicure's paradise, I knew I would enjoy its many prehistoric archaeological sites. Before I'd left for France I'd spent a lot of time reading up on aspects of the country that might make interesting research projects for my television programs, and I'd been particularly interested in the Périgord because of its famous caves.

Périgord was, after all, the place where the first skeletal remains of a type of early man, known as Cro-Magnon man, had come to light a little over a hundred years ago—in 1868, to be exact. Scientists had been particularly excited at the discovery since, unlike Neanderthal man, the remains hardly differ from modern man. Indeed, the Cro-Magnon men might well be our ancestors. The name derived from Cro-Magnon, on the edge of a village called Les Eyzies, and gradually, as research progressed, a whole prehistoric civilization had come to light. This early human society, centered in southwest France, dated back as far as 40,000 years ago. I remembered that the archaeologists had been interested by the care with which the Cro-Magnon people had colored their dead with red ocher and buried them in shallow graves, probably believing, as many of us still do, in the immortality of the soul.

Then had come the sensational discovery, by four boys in 1940, of the caves of Lascaux—huge grottoes filled with the most beautiful prehistoric art. The caves have been nicknamed the Sistine Chapel of Prehistory, and decorated with mural paintings of animals. Bulls are the largest figures, but deer and horses are also commonly represented, and there are fine engravings, as well. I remember from my reading that some scientists think that the caves were sanctuaries laid out according to a set pattern—for example, certain combinations of animals, such as bison and horses, were required—but this was only a theory. I would have liked to have seen the caves for myself, but I knew they'd been closed to the public since 1960, when it was noticed that the spread of algae was causing the paintings to deteriorate. Well, I would just have to be satisfied to visit the famous prehistoric museum in nearby Les Eyzies.

That evening as I was lying in my bed, exhausted after a day of battling the hustle and bustle of a great metropolis, there was a knock on the door. Surprised, I got up to open it and found a bellboy standing there. "Telegram for you, miss," he said.

I tipped him, closed the door and tore open the envelope. Inside was a telegram from Norman: "Be a sweetheart, little sister. Find Maurice wherever he is. Urge him to come to see me. Love, Norman."

That did it. The following day I put some of my bulkier suitcases into storage. Taking the rest of my luggage with me, I checked out of the hotel room and headed for the railway station. I would spend the summer in the Périgord and return to Paris in the fall. I felt carefree and happy, like a schoolgirl who's just finished her term and is about to embark on her first long voyage on her own. *Who knows what lies ahead of me*, I thought.

Chapter 2

I found myself comfortably settled in one of the compartments of *La Capitole*, the luxury train that does the run from Paris to the southwest corner of France. There was really something quite charming, I thought, about this old-fashioned French habit of giving names to their first-class trains. I particularly liked the name of *Le Capitole's* sister train to Marseille the Riviera: it was called *Le Mistral* after the cold north wind that blows over the Midi, as the southern part of France is generally called. I remembered that the mistral had figured prominently in many of the romantic novels I'd read that were set in that region.

All these thoughts conjured up the good old days of train travel—the *Orient Express* . . . mystery . . . romance. I had to laugh a little at myself for letting my imagination run riot, but I was genuinely excited at the thought of what strange adventures might be awaiting me at my destination.

By the time I changed trains at Limoges and finally arrived at Périgueux, the principal city of the Périgord, it was already late in the evening. I was much too tired to hunt around the sleeping city for a place to stay, and was thus grateful to find a room in the hotel across the street from the station. It was a large room, beautifully decorated with Renaissance furniture that looked authentic. Sinking gratefully into the big, four-poster bed, I fell into a dreamless sleep.

The next morning I surveyed myself critically in the mirror; I decided that the previous night's rest had done wonders for my appearance. My violent blue eyes had recovered their lively sparkle, my long, honey-colored hair looked shinier than it had in days.

Feeling completely refreshed, I took a leisurely tour around the city. My guide was one of the local taxi drivers who was both enthusiastic and knowledgeable about all the marvels that Périgueux had to offer. His pride in his hometown was, I thought, eminently justifiable: I was enchanted with the city.

"That was built by the Romans," he told me as we passed the ruins of a large oval amphitheater. "This city's been inhabited ever since the days of the Roman Empire, but it was known as Vesunna back then and was an important town of Gaul." He went on to explain that after the fall of the Roman Empire, it sank into relative obscurity until the Middle Ages. Then it flourished once more and was now full of architectural treasures from that period.

As we drove through the streets of the old city, I realized that Périgueux really deserved its reputation as a city of art. Everywhere, I saw magnificent old Gothic houses with beautifully carved stone stairways. Here and there among them, there were more recent Renaissance-style buildings, with loggias and porticoes in the best Italian manner, some dating back to the sixteenth century.

Getting out of the cab at one point, I ventured for a short time along the narrow side streets, following their twists and turns, pausing to look in the myriad antique shops that lined each side. The turreted houses, I felt, were stone poems that spoke to me, in a mysterious and fascinating language, of the history of old France.

Returning to my cab and driver, I went on to the local archaeological museum, where a splendid collection of prehistoric artifacts recalled the much more ancient and even more mysterious world of Cro-Magnon man. By this time, I realized that I'd fallen in love with the Périgord, and I knew it would take me a long time to savor all the delights that it had to offer. I promised myself to stay in the area as long as possible.

"By the way," I said, suddenly remembering the original purpose of my trip, "where can I find Delacour Manor?"

The driver reached over to the glove compartment of the car and pulled out a map. With his help, I picked out the place where, according to his old concierge, Maurice Briançon was supposed to be living. "Delacour Manor is about fifteen miles from here," he said, tracing the route on the map with a ball-point pen.

"Can you take me there?" I asked.

Unfortunately he wasn't free: he'd been hired for the afternoon by some tourists who wanted to visit the local châteaus.

I decided to rent a car and drive there myself. After all, I thought, I'd decided to settle down here for a while, and I might as well be able to get around as I pleased. The Périgord contained all kinds of fascinating architectural and archaeological treasures that I wanted to see, and I was eager to begin my voyage of discovery.

Without further ado, I went to one of the car-rental agencies and rented a sturdy-looking little Renault, and while I was there I obtained a detailed road map of the area, as well as a gourmet's guide. I didn't want to miss out on the many Périgord country inns that were renowned for their fine cuisine. With my trusty camera placed on the seat beside me, I drove off in search of adventure.

I drove out along the Isle River, whose still dark waters mirrored the tall trees that lined its banks. It was a beautiful early-May afternoon. The sky was bright and the trees in full bloom. In fact I was somewhat surprised to see that their tender, translucent leaves had already grown so much. In Canada the vegetation wasn't nearly as advanced at this time of year. As I continued my drive, I met with one enchanting vista after another. Here and there, among the vineyards and tidy orchards that also bordered the river I saw the white flocks of sheep and geese for which the area is famous. The overall impression was one of quiet, pastoral serenity, and I was imbued with a feeling of tremendous peace and contentment.

I stopped for a late lunch at the small town of Mussidan, about twenty-five miles down the river from Périgueux. At the local restaurant, I had my first taste of two regional delicacies—stuffed neck of goose and truffles roasted over hot coals. I obtained the recipes for these succulent dishes from an obliging chef, knowing that my friend Mary, who produced cooking shows for CBC Radio, would be only too delighted to have them.

As I was finishing off a delicious chocolate mousse and having a cup of rich, strong coffee, I began to think about where I would stay for the night. I'd become a bit more hesitant about my visit to Maurice since I'd learned he was married and realized that I couldn't just arrive at his place with all my stuff and invite myself to stay overnight. He had his own family life, perhaps even children, and I had no desire to appear unexpectedly and barge in, obliging them to put me up.

I drove slowly back along the river and was still pondering the choices open to me when I came to the small town of Neuvic. A glance at the map assured me it was the largest village in the vicinity of Delacour Manor, and as I noticed a sign on one of the houses, I suddenly realized how to solve my problem. In neat hand-lettered script, the sign read: Rental agency. Your choice of châteaus, villas, country houses.

A pleasant young woman greeted me with a broad smile as I walked into the agency. I explained to her that I was looking for some place nearby where I could stay for the summer.

"Are you looking for something fancy?" the woman asked.

"No, not at all. But I'd like to find a place with some character at least."

She looked through her files. Suddenly, her eyes lighted up. "I think I have just the place for you," she said. "It's a small place on the river near the dam, where the lock keeper used to live. It's not in use now, because the lock's no longer working. Some people from Paris bought it and fixed it up, but they're not coming down this year, so they're renting it out. You can have it for the whole summer if you like."

"It sounds perfect," I exclaimed excitedly, particularly pleased by the idea of living beside the water.

The rental agent took me to look at the house. It was a small stone cottage on an acre or so of land, surrounded by pine trees and almost hidden by the profusion of wild flowers that grew all around it. From the outside it had an air of romantic neglect that appealed to me immediately. When we went inside, I was equally delighted to find that the interior had been beautifully renovated, furnished in the best of taste and equipped with all the modern conveniences. A floating bridge connected the cottage to a small island, and I saw a flat-bottomed boat moored alongside.

"Is the boat also for rent?" I asked.

"No, it belongs to the people who own the château across the way. But I could easily get one for you, if you like."

Opposite the lock keeper's house, on the other side of the river, stood a large, medieval château. Like a moving mirror the dark waters of the Isle reflected its crenellated towers. Its splendid proportions made it both majestic and charming.

"That's the Château Donazac," the agent said. "There's a village of the same name just down the road, where you can do your grocery shopping."

By now I was sold on the place. "When can I move in?" I asked.

"Tomorrow, if you like. Just give us a little time to make a list of the contents, and fix up the rooms that haven't been used all winter. I'll get Emma, one of the local women, to take care of it. You can also get her to help you with the housework, if you want to."

Although it didn't solve my overnight problem, the lock keeper's house seemed to be just what I was looking for, and I was sure I could find a room in an inn somewhere nearby. When we got back to the agency, I signed a four-month lease. As I placed my signature at the bottom of the official-looking paper, it suddenly struck me that I'd really taken possession of a house. At long last I felt that I'd finally put down roots in the soil of France, a country so dear to my heart. I was very happy, in particular, to be settling down in the Périgord, which I'd been told was one of the most beautiful regions of France. Certainly my drive that afternoon had done nothing to convince me otherwise. I was sure that I would find plenty of useful material for my TV programs in this particular area alone, to say nothing of other regions in the country.

All these arrangements with the house had taken up quite a bit of time. It was already late afternoon and I wanted to let Maurice know that I had arrived. As I left the rental office, I saw a telephone booth a little way down the street. I went over to it and flipped through the directory, only to discover, to my great disappointment, that Delacour Manor either didn't have a telephone or had an unlisted number. That was a pity;

however, as I wasn't far from the manor I thought I'd just drive over and say hello.

I studied the lines that my Périgueux taxi driver had so helpfully penned on my map. Full of optimism, I followed the river road for a few miles, then turned onto a secondary road. This, I found, wound along beside a cliff for some distance, then plunged suddenly and unexpectedly into a dense forest. A few minutes later, I caught glimpses through the trees of the ruins of a large building, perched high on a hillside. Crumbling turrets and the half-ruined shape of a columned gallery were outlined against the sky. Shortly thereafter, I came across a rough dirt road branching off in the direction of the ruins, and beside it, a faded sign that bore the legend, The Abbot's House. I was tempted to make a detour to have a look. I felt drawn to these relics of a forgotten architecture, which, in my romantic youthfulness, I regarded as far superior to so much of the modern stuff. But the road was pretty rough, and I wasn't sure that my little Renault could negotiate it. Besides, I also realized that I didn't have any time to spare at that particular moment.

I continued on my way. Around me, the forest grew thicker and darker, the branches of the impressively tall, ancient trees blocking out the bright, late-afternoon sun. As its cheerful light and warmth disappeared, so, little by little, did my confidence. The road was now little more than a track, and as I bumped along it I felt a sudden rush of anxiety. *Perhaps I've taken a wrong turn*, I thought. But I was soon reassured by an ancient sign that said Delacour Manor. An arrow pointed to a shadowy driveway lined with oaks and chestnut trees.

I ventured onto the driveway. My wheels sunk into deep ruts, and I had to drive along for a few minutes before I saw, literally buried in the midst of green, exuberant vegetation, the gray towers of an imposing, yet vaguely forbidding, residence.

Delacour Manor was reminiscent of a bygone era, but what struck me particularly, as I stopped and got out of the car, was the silence and solitude of the place. I wondered if Maurice could really be living in this fortress, which looked like a stage set for some medieval romance.

The high, half-ruined castle keep was almost hidden by a dense mantle of ivy, pierced here and there with narrow loopholes. I thought I could almost see the scratches left on these lethal slits by the crossbows that had once poked out to rain death on the enemies below.

Impressed and not a little nervous, I took a turn around the manor. No, I thought, I really hadn't expected to encounter such a setting, at once so romantic, mysterious and wild, which the tall dark trees seemed to be guarding, like so many men-at-arms. I remembered that as a child, I had imagined the castle of Sleeping Beauty to be just such a place.

I continued my inspection, feeling somewhat intimidated by the spirit of the place. My feet squished on dead, wet leaves, and from time to time I stumbled on stones hidden in the grass. The silence was so complete that it seemed unreal. In fact, I began to wonder whether anyone lived there at all, until I noticed a cow grazing peacefully in a meadow obviously carved out of the forest many years before. It was the first living creature I'd seen in this enchanted wood, and it was with a feeling of relief that I realized there were people living here after all.

Indeed, on the side of the building that faced the meadow, the feeling of isolation disappeared altogether. The walls had been pierced by a number of casement windows—probably in Renaissance times—and a door had been recessed between two carved pilasters of the facade. The windows were decorated with curtains. At last, I had found some evidence of human life and warmth. By now I was fully alert, and restless with curiosity and impatience. I walked over to ring the doorbell, which echoed hollowly in the depths of the manor. After a few moments, the door opened slightly and the inquisitive face of an old woman servant peered out at me.

A bit taken aback, I apologized for my unexpected intrusion.

"Excuse me. I didn't meet anyone in the driveway or on the grounds. Could I see Mr. Briançon?"

The woman looked at me blankly, as if she didn't understand a word I was saying. I wondered if she spoke only the local dialect, and perhaps I'd lost my way after all. "This is Delacour Manor, isn't it?" I asked anxiously in what I knew to be perfectly respectable, though by no means flawless, French.

She nodded her head, still staring at me. Her face remained expressionless beneath the dark gray headscarf that was wound around her wrinkled face.

"Then it is the residence of Mr. Briançon?" I insisted.

She said nothing, but continued to stare at me, her face now taking on a strange expression of suspicion. She seemed to be trying to figure out who I was, and why I'd come. *Well*, I thought, *I'm certainly not going to give Maurice high marks for the kind of welcome he provides for visitors to his abode.* But then I realized people obviously weren't accustomed to having many visitors in this area.

"What do you want?" she said at last. She had a rough, grating accent with a slight lilt to it.

"I'd like to see Mr. Briançon," I replied, considering my patience admirable under the circumstances.

"Who?"

She must be deaf, I thought in exasperation. Then suddenly her expression changed. Her eyelids fluttered and she looked like some startled bird.

A moment later, coming from the hallway a voice asked, "What is it, Lucy?"

The old woman turned around quickly and murmured a few words that I didn't understand. The voice uttered an exclamation, and all at once another figure appeared at Lucy's side. It was a young woman, the smooth milk-white complexion of her face accentuated by the raven-black hair drawn tightly back into a bun. She was, I realized, extraordinarily beautiful, but in a cold, almost statuelike way. She turned to gaze at me inquisitively, with no hint of warmth or welcome showing in her green eyes.

I was about to explain my presence, but she spoke first. "Who did you say you were looking for?" she asked cautiously.

"Mr. Briançon."

Her mouth twitched. Her face, as perfect in its regularity as a Madonna in a stained-glass window, assumed an air of disbelief. "Maurice!" she exclaimed. "But who are you?"

She looked me over in a dignified, severe way, motionless on the threshold, as if she were trying to defend it. The unrelenting coldness of her reception was almost more than I could bear, and I had an almost irresistable urge to turn around and leave.

Instead I answered her question with one of my own. "Would you be his wife?"

"Who are you?" she said again abruptly, apparently annoyed by my intrusion.

"Dawn Charbonneau," I replied rather sharply, my patience beginning to wear a little thin. "I'm from Canada, from Montreal. My brother, Norman, wrote Maurice to tell him I was coming."

The young woman took a deep breath then sighed, seemingly with relief. "Ah! I see," she said. "Well, I'm Alys Briançon, and yes, I'm Maurice's wife."

For a second we looked at one another. The formalities and introduction finally over, I gave her a halfhearted smile in an attempt to be friendly. Considering how annoyed I still was, the smile probably looked a little forced, but surely it warranted more than I received from Maurice's wife. She gave no sign of acknowledgement, but simply continued to stand silently and coldly in the half-open doorway.

"I did try to telephone you, because I didn't want to show up unannounced like this," I said at last, feeling decidedly intimidated. "But I couldn't find any number in the phone book. I was hoping to get in touch with Maurice before—"

I got no further. Suddenly interrupting my explanation, she announced in a flat tone, "My husband is dead, Mademoiselle Charbonneau."

Chapter 3

For a moment I simply stared at her in disbelief. "Maurice . . . is dead?" I managed to stammer finally. "But that's not possible!"

My outburst was followed by a long silence that only emphasized the foolishness of my protest. Finally Alys said, "I'm sorry that you didn't know. It happened only a short time ago."

"Oh, I . . . I'm so sorry. Excuse me, I . . . ." Frankly, I didn't know what to say. The situation was so totally unexpected that I was at a complete loss for words.

"Please come in," she said, suddenly finding her manners and stepping back into the hallway.

I followed her into the broad entrance hall and then on into an immense drawing room. An enormous fireplace took up most of the wall at one end of the room, which was lighted by three tall windows hung with heavy, burgundy-colored velvet drapes.

Politely Alys offered me an armchair and sat down in another opposite me. "You must excuse my hesitation in welcoming you," she said, "but I was completely unprepared for your visit. Since I've been in mourning, I've hardly received any visitors at all."

For the first time, I noticed the severe black dress she was wearing, and the jet necklace that glittered at her throat. On her the whole outfit looked so elegant and natural that it had never occurred to me that it was anything other than the way she normally dressed. Desperately I hunted for the right words to suit the occasion. "I'm terribly sorry to hear that Maurice is dead," I murmured at last. "Norman is going to be very saddened when he hears the news: he loved Maurice like a brother. I suppose that your husband had spoken to you about us?"

She nodded, but remained silent. Her sharp green eyes were fastened on me and she was obviously still very wary of my presence. Her attitude was disturbing, to say the least, and I felt very ill at ease.

"How . . . did it happen?" I managed to stammer. "He was so young, and when I knew him he was very strong and in the pink of health."

Daintily Alys rubbed her hands against her temples. It was an affected gesture that seemed oddly out of keeping with her appearance. Although beautifully slender, she didn't look the least bit delicate or helpless—quite the opposite, in fact; she appeared to have all the lithe grace of a cat, and I suspected a steely strength under that cold, perfectly composed exterior.

Pointedly she avoided answering my question. With her eyes averted she murmured, "He was forty-three. Yes, it's young. Death ought not to have taken him so soon."

"Especially at the beginning of a new life. . . . "

She raised her head suddenly and looked at me in surprise. "A new life?" she echoed sharply.

"He'd left Paris, hadn't he, and moved back to the family estate? That's what they told me at rue Jacob, when I went to his gallery."

"Yes, that's true," she admitted. "We'd just settled down at Delacour: Maurice had inherited it. He had always enjoyed it here and detested Paris. So, as soon as he could get away from the city, he did. Well, that's the story."

She spread her hands in a gesture of distress. My embarrassment increased and I stammered my apologies. "I'm . . . terribly sorry that I've reminded you of your grief. I wouldn't have come if my brother hadn't insisted so much. It was really because of Maurice's letter."

"Maurice's letter?" she queried quickly, almost sharply, straightening suddenly in her chair. Her eyes took that same wary look they had when she came to the door.

"He wrote to my brother to say he planned to come to Canada," I explained, somewhat taken aback by her reaction.

After all, I thought, *she is his wife, or rather, his widow, to be more exact. I have no reason not to tell her that Maurice had reestablished contact with his Canadian friends.* As I explained the circumstances that had brought me to Delacour Manor, Alys listened intently. Her eyes never wavered from my face, and I received the uncomfortable impression that she was judging the accuracy of my story from the expressions it held. Her own face remained devoid of all expression, and I couldn't tell whether she believed my words or not, but from time to time she nodded her head slightly, to show that she was following what I was saying.

Refusing to be intimidated, I plowed resolutely on, describing all the problems I'd encountered at her husband's club and the gallery on rue Jacob. As I reached the end of my story she sank back in her chair, and I sensed, rather than saw, her feeling of relief. Before either of us had time to say a word, a familiar sound penetrated the thick walls of the mansion from the courtyard outside—two brief honks of a car horn. I heard a car door slam shut.

Alys quickly got to her feet. "Please excuse me for a moment," she said.

Moving rapidly, she seemed to glide across the room, her high heels barely making a sound on the polished floor. *Yes*, I thought, *she really is a very beautiful woman.* And I had to admit to myself that I admired her for dressing so elegantly, despite the fact she had apparently decided to spend her period of mourning in solitude, in this remote place. Her dress looked like a Dior or a St. Laurent, and the black pearl that glistened on her finger must have been worth a small fortune.

Maurice, I supposed, must have made plenty of money selling paintings, to be able to give his wife such expensive jewelry.

I heard the front door open. Then heavy footsteps sounded in the hallway, which were joined by the lighter ones of Alys. Expecting to see several visitors appear in the drawing room at any moment, I sat up straighter in my formal, high-backed armchair.

I needn't have bothered, for no one came into the room. Out in the hallway a conversation began, and I couldn't help overhearing a few words now and then through the door that Alys had left partially open.

Her visitor was obviously a man, for the first voice I heard was deep and unpleasantly guttural. The few words I caught were so unexpected my curiosity was instantly aroused, and unashamedly I strained to hear more. ". . . came to warn you," he said. ". . . escaped."

"Escaped?" Alys echoed quickly, her voice high-pitched in sudden alarm.

" . . . come later tonight," remarked her visitor.

I held my breath, waiting for him to continue, but at that point Alys must have warned him that she had company. His voice dropped to little more than a whisper and I could hear no more. However, the tone and words of the parts of the conversation I had heard had been enough to awaken my journalistic instincts. There was a story here somewhere, of that I was sure, and I wondered what it could be.

A few moments later I gave up my idle speculations. I hadn't heard enough to have obtained any real clues, and besides, I told myself sternly, it was really none of my business, anyway.

A short time later I heard the front door slam, then a car engine springing to life and the subsequent hiss of tires rolling over the dry earth of the driveway. Alys came back into the drawing room, alone, her face creased in a worried frown.

I got up quickly. "I hope I'm not inconveniencing you. I mean, if there's something bothering you . . ." I began.

For a moment she seemed surprised by my presence, as though she'd forgotten I was there. Then her face cleared, and with a wave of her hand she cut short my polite protests. "Oh, don't worry," she said. "This doesn't have anything to do with you. I told you that I haven't wanted to receive visitors lately."

Well, you have a strange way of showing it, I thought, *inviting that man into the hallway and engaging in a decidedly odd conversation.*

Alys and I exchanged a few words, but the atmosphere remained strained.

"I'm going to make some tea," she said abruptly. "If you'd like some, that is."

I accepted her offer and for form's sake added, "I hope I'm not putting you to any trouble."

"Not at all," Alys replied politely. As she got up and went out to make the tea herself, she apologized for leaving me alone. "Lucy's one of the locals and she's never learned how to make tea properly," she explained. "As far as Lucy's concerned, it's just a medicine." Unexpectedly Alys gave a little laugh. It was an odd, dry laugh: a false note in the harmony of her otherwise smooth, polished, but highly impersonal, manners.

Alys, I thought, was not a name that suited either her surroundings or her marblelike coldness. She reminded me in some ways of a lady in a Gothic romance, and she inspired in me a strange mixture of curiosity, pity and something closely akin to dislike. She was young, but her life had already been marred by tragedy. And all around her was this awful solitude that threatened to engulf even the most misanthropic of individuals. She didn't strike me as someone who would enjoy living in such loneliness—quite the opposite, in fact, for I could well imagine her gracing the ballrooms and theaters of Paris, provocative and sensual, reveling in the attention her beauty was bound to inspire in any hapless young man present at such functions. And I couldn't help but wonder what kept her in this lonely spot.

I got up and walked over to one of the casement windows. As I gazed abstractedly at the vast panorama of the forest that hemmed in the ancient manor on all sides, I felt a touch of claustrophobia. Forests always have this effect on me: I like them, but as soon as I'm in the middle of them, I have the unpleasant sensation of being a prisoner.

I examined the grounds near the house, struck by the absence of any garden. The large, leafy chestnut tree, the well and the clump of elm trees seemed to be the only attempts at landscaping. If I'd lived there I knew I'd have wanted to surround myself with flowers to lessen the severity of the environment.

Looking more closely, however, I discovered some boxwood trees, a thicket of yew trees and what had probably once been a rose garden, but which now was reduced to nothing more than a few scraggly shrubs. The fact that my hostess hadn't even made any attempt to restore what had, at one time, perhaps been a beautiful garden, only served to confirm my impression that she had no real desire to remain here.

At that point my reflections were interrupted by Alys, who came into the room pushing a small trolley in front of her. For some reason she now seemed very nervous. In fact, her hand trembled so much as she poured the tea into my cup that she spilled a few drops onto the saucer.

"Oh! Excuse me," she exclaimed, her action somewhat excessive considering the triviality of the incident, or so I thought.

We drank in silence. It seemed that we had nothing more to say to one another. I felt decidedly uncomfortable, and somewhat sadly thought to myself that if Maurice had been there everything would have been different. He'd have welcomed me warmly and insisted on my staying, I was sure.

As if she guessed something of my thoughts, Alys set her empty cup down on the trolley and asked, "You've already visited the Périgord?"

"No, not yet," I replied. "I'm planning to take my time about it."

"You're going to stay here?" A touch of wariness had crept into her voice and she averted her eyes, as if fearful that I was about to settle down right then and there, in her own home.

Surely, I thought, *she doesn't think that I'm trying to cadge an invitation to move into Delacour Manor?* I hastened to assure her I had no such intention. "I've already rented a small house nearby," I explained. "I thought I was going to meet Maurice, and I'd have been pleased to be his neighbor."

She gave me a brief, impersonal smile, but said nothing more.

She really is completely lacking in human warmth, I thought rather crossly. *Just to be polite, she could at least have said that I am as welcome to stay in her house now as I would have been when her husband was alive.*

I looked at my watch and got up. "It's time for me to be going," I said. "My little cottage won't be ready until tomorrow and I have to look for a place to stay for the night."

Still she said nothing. By that time, even if she *had* offered to let me stay for the one night, I wouldn't have accepted. She was too reserved, too lacking in basic hospitality, for me to feel at all comfortable or easy in her presence. No doubt it was a question of temperament, or perhaps it was her mourning that made her so unsociable.

But then, apparently feeling a belated remorse, she halfheartedly suggested, "Wouldn't you like to stay for dinner?"

"Thank you, but I really must leave now," I replied. "I might not be able to find a room if I stayed on."

There was no doubt in my mind that Alys was relieved at my refusal. I pulled on my coat, and she escorted me out to my car. We said goodbye, both of us clearly relieved the meeting was over.

I got into my little Renault and pressed on the starter. Nothing happened. I tried again several times, but met with the same lack of success.

Alys came over. "Is something wrong?" she asked, and I thought I detected a note of anxiety in her voice.

I looked at her blankly. I was dumbfounded and felt a tiny surge of panic. "It seems so," I said at last. "It won't start."

I repeated my efforts, at first methodically, then feverishly. The car obstinately refused to work. Angrily, I redoubled my efforts.

"It must be the battery," Alys declared with apparent authority.

"You know something about cars?" I asked hopefully.

She gave a little laugh and declared emphatically, "Absolutely nothing. I don't even know how to drive." Bitterly she added, "Maurice never let me touch a steering wheel. And since his death I just don't seem to have got around to learning. . . ."

I climbed out and stared at the Renault in perplexity. "Now what?" I exclaimed angrily, completely frustrated. I didn't know what to do.

"We can give you a push, if you like," Alys suggested.

"It might work," I conceded doubtfully. "It's worth a try, anyway."

Alys went over to an old building at the side of the house. In the shadows of the open doorway, half-hidden by bales of straw, I could make out the indistinct shapes of farm machinery. She spoke to someone inside the shed, and an old man emerged. Pointing to the car, she explained what was expected of him. As he walked over, he spat on his hands and wiped them off on his cord trousers.

The old man, whom Alys called Ambrose, then examined the Renault suspiciously. Quite obviously he'd never driven a car in his life, maybe not even a tractor. "We'll have a go at it," he said timidly.

I got back in the car. Ambrose started to push, helped by Alys. As the car started to roll, I let in the clutch and the motor coughed. The vehicle went ahead a few yards then stopped again, and I had the distinct impression that this time it had stopped for good.

Discouraged, I turned back to look at my helpers. "There's no more juice," I said in a voice full of chagrin. "I'm afraid I'm stuck."

Ambrose looked completely worn out. Alys, red faced and with her hair awry, smoothed her locks back into place.

"Now what do I do?" I asked despairingly.

Chapter 4

Alys threw up her arms in a gesture of depair and shook her head. "I don't really know," she replied, completely at a loss. She looked up at the sky where the last pink clouds of sunset were fading into twilight. "It's getting dark," she said unnecessarily. "It will soon be night, and it's a good ten miles from here to Neuvic."

"You don't have any means of transportation, I suppose?" I inquired with a sinking feeling.

"Tony, the old man's son, has a small motor bike for running errands in town for us. But he won't be back until later this evening. He went to Périgueux for the day. Do you know how to ride a motorbike?"

I admitted I didn't. I could drive a Mercedes and even my tricky Renault—when it was running—but I'd never been on a motorcycle in my life. And I didn't intend to start now.

"Well, then, we'll have to wait until Tony gets back: he can take a message to town," Alys concluded, obviously as rattled as I was by this unfortunate turn of events. "He went off with one of the farmers. I imagine he'll be back quite late—he usually is, on his day off—so there's no point in expecting him home for several hours."

"By which time the rental agency will be closed," I murmured. Once more I looked at my car in disgust, silently cursing the agent who'd given me this jalopy and put me in such an embarrassing position.

After a brief silence Alys said, "I'm afraid you have no alternative but to spend the night here."

She could at least have tried to sound as though she might enjoy the company for a change, I thought angrily. "I wouldn't dream of it," I replied stiffly. "I don't want to put you to any trouble."

"Well, then?" That was all Alys could manage. She didn't seem capable of saying, as common courtesy required, that I wouldn't be putting her to any trouble at all; that I should make myself at home. She was being almost unbelievably inhospitable, and in fact seemed thoroughly annoyed by the whole thing.

I could neither understand, nor accept, her attitude. After all, this was Maurice's home and Maurice would have shown me every courtesy. I found it hard to believe that he could have chosen to marry a woman as lacking in common decency as Alys appeared to be at this moment. Surely there had to be some reason for her strange and hostile attitude. . . . Once again my journalistic instincts came to the fore, and I had a sudden desire to try to find out what that reason was. *This lady,* I thought grimly, *is going to fulfill her duties as a hostess whether she likes it or not.*

"Well, then?" Alys repeated.

I pretended to think it over, but I'd already made up my mind. "Well, then," I declared at last and with feigned reluctance, "there doesn't seem to be any other solution. So I accept your kind offer. But please accept my apologies for the unexpected intrusion."

She bit her lip. "It's my fault for living out here in the middle of nowhere," she said savagely. "This place is as remote from civilization as a hut in the middle of a jungle."

She shrugged, then turned her back on me. As she strode toward the house, she called over her shoulder, "I'm going to have your room made ready. Ambrose will bring in your suitcase."

I opened the trunk of the car and took out the small traveling case that contained everything I needed for an overnight stay. Then, accompanied by the aged Ambrose, I caught up with Alys, who was standing by the front door conferring with Lucy.

As I came up she turned toward me. "It's ridiculous not to have a telephone these days," she sighed. "You may find it hard to believe that we don't have one, but it's very expensive to have a line strung all the way out here, and you have to wait for ages for the work to be done. Maurice's grandmother never bothered with a phone, but then, she lived here at Delacour the way people lived a hundred years ago, without any modern conveniences."

I was astounded at Alys's sudden talkativeness, and equally astounded at the strength of the bitterness that edged her voice.

"When we first moved in here, we found that we didn't even have running water. Modern plumbing has only been installed within the last six months. Maurice was having the place properly wired, too. It's mostly done now, though there are a few rooms upstairs still without lights." Alys waved her hand in a vague gesture of helplessness.

Having come to terms with the situation, I now felt pleased that I'd have the chance to live, for a few hours at least, in such an unusual and romantic environment. On the eve of my departure for France, I'd never have dreamed that I'd be staying in such an old-fashioned place as Delacour Manor, where time seemed to have stood still.

A moment or so later, Alys took me upstairs and showed me into an enormous room at the end of a short corridor leading off from the right of the staircase. "You'll sleep here," she said politely. "I hope you find it comfortable." Obviously she'd decided to make the best of this misfortune and had managed to recover at least a semblance of good manners, impersonal though they were.

"The bathroom is next door," she continued. "It's as old-fashioned as the rest of the place, I'm afraid, and I apologize for it. Please make yourself at home and relax. We'll have dinner at eight o'clock."

Though there was evidence of new plumbing in the bathroom, little else by way of modernization and re-decoration had been carried out. The room was, in fact, in need of a rather major face-lift. Still, I was imbued with a certain sense of adventure, and after freshening up I descended a little before eight to rejoin my hostess.

Immediately and without a word she led the way into the dining room. Apart from the large chandelier in the middle of the room, there were several candelabra that lined the walls and framed the huge fireplace. The flickering light shone softly on the pewter, the heavy silver and the patina of the old furniture. The whole scene was fantastic and somehow unreal.

"I feel as if I'm living in a fairy tale," I said to Alys as I took my place across from her on one side of the long, carved oak table, where we both seemed a bit lost. "I had no idea that these extraordinary medieval manor houses still existed."

"There are plenty of places like this around here," she replied, pushing the heavy silver soup tureen toward me. "Some are completely ruined. Others are still inhabited, even year round, but their owners—thank God—have fixed them up so they can live in them like normal human beings. They have central heating and TV."

"Somehow, I feel that TV would be out of place in one of these old houses," I remarked, ladling some thick pea soup into my bowl.

She looked at me, mockery in her eyes. "I'd just like to see you try to live in this place for a while," she said. "It's all very well to make a cult of the past, but if you have to live the way people really did in the Middle Ages, you'd soon become disillusioned, believe me. Things have changed a lot since the days of the Crusaders, you know; we're all terribly addicted to our modern comforts."

"Well," I replied with a smile, "considering the way you feel about it, I'm really surprised that you've shut yourself up in this . . . this Sleeping Beauty's castle."

She averted her eyes. "I have my reasons," she murmured quietly. "But you can be sure that if I could do whatever I wanted, I wouldn't hang around this prison for long."

Once again I wondered what was holding her back. After all, she was a grown woman and presumably could do as she pleased. Obviously there had to be some extraordinary set of circumstances that forced her to lead this solitary life, which she clearly didn't care for, but I couldn't even begin to imagine what they might be.

We spoke of other things. Alys asked me about my brother and our life in Canada. She deliberately avoided talking about Maurice, and when I made a couple of attempts to steer the conversation around to the subject of her late husband, I ran into a wall of silence. Perhaps, I thought, she didn't feel strong enough to deal with such a painful subject. After all, it hadn't been that long since he'd died and she was still in mourning.

Lucy served us coffee in the drawing room. I looked around again at the massive pieces of furniture, the ancestral portraits, the grand piano and the medieval fireplace. My knowledge of antiques was very limited, but even I could tell that at least a few of the pieces were of museum quality.

One of the many paintings caught my eye. It was a portrait, set high above the massive fireplace, and in the dancing flame of the candles it almost seemed to come to life. "Is that Maurice's father?" I asked.

"No, a distant cousin, Roland Laurensac. He went off to live in Mexico." With a slight smile of disdain she added, "The painting is quite unremarkable—mediocre in all aspects."

Mediocre or not I liked it, but then I really knew very little about art. However, I did wonder why the likeness of some distant cousin should be given such a prominent place in the main room of the house.

Alys offered me a cigarette from a large silver box and took one herself. The conversation languished as we smoked. My hostess looked as preoccupied and remote as ever. In fact, I was beginning to wonder how on earth we were going to get through the evening, considering we had so little in common, when, as if reading my thoughts, she said, "Forgive me for being such poor company, but I'm in the habit of retiring early. I hope you won't mind if I leave you now, but I've got a bit of a headache and—"

"Please, don't apologize," I replied, getting to my feet. "I should be the one who's apologizing, for keeping you up." I had no desire to force her to alter her habits in any way simply for my benefit. Moreover, I, too, was beginning to see the virtues of calling it a day.

As I said good-night to Alys, she pointed to a pile of magazines on a side table and suggested that I take one or two up with me to read before going to sleep. I declined her offer, being confident that after such a hectic day I was going to fall asleep very quickly.

As soon as I got back to my candle-lighted bedroom, however—sure enough, mine was one of the rooms the electrician hadn't got around to—I began to regret that I hadn't accepted Alys's offer of a magazine or two to read. I had been far too hasty in assuming that I would drop off immediately; in fact, I was surprisingly restless.

I put my things away by the flickering light of the tall

candelabrum on top of the dresser. Lucy had also lighted
the wall brackets and placed a candlestick on my bedside
table. *They must go through an exceptional number of
candles in this house*, I thought to myself.

As I walked around the room blowing out the candles
one by one, I went over the events of the day, trying to
pin down the source of the vague sense of uneasiness
that had gradually been creeping over me. I'd experienced shock at the news of Maurice's death, annoyance at the breakdown of my car and irritation at
Alys's cold reception. But there was also someting else—
an indescribable but persistent feeling that something
was wrong. It wasn't anything I could put my finger on,
but the incongruity of Alys living in this isolated spot
continued to prey on my mind, and I sensed a mystery
not far beneath the surface.

I'd been so happy that morning, so optimistic and
carefree. Now I began to feel sorry that I'd rented the
house beside the river. I'd counted on having friends in
the area to make my stay a pleasant one, but Alys's inhospitality certainly put paid to that idea. *Well*, I
thought, *I'll just have to wait and see what happens*.

I climbed into the high canopied bed, which made me
feel rather like a princess of olden times. Norman, I
knew, would have to be informed of Maurice's death,
and if I knew my brother, he'd want as many details as
possible. I didn't really have much to tell him so far, but
decided to write him at least a short note in the morning. In my mind, I turned over the sentences that
would comprise my letter, but I reached the end of my
narrative without managing to put myself to sleep.

The house was silent. Somewhere a clock ticked.
Outside, I heard for a brief instant the cry of an owl.
Rapidly becoming fed up with tossing and turning in my
bed, I struck a match and lighted the bedside candle. I
decided to go downstairs and pick up a couple of the

magazines Alys had offered me, hoping that if I read for a while, I'd be able to get to sleep.

I jumped down out of the bed and put on my slippers and dressing gown. With muffled steps, I made my way along the corridor and down the stairs, carrying my candlestick in front of me.

Silently I eased open the door that led into the large drawing room. To my surprise, it was partially illumined with shafts of silver light. The curtains had only been half drawn across the high windows and a full moon, now risen, shone brightly through the gaps between them. Uneasily I peered around the room. The center portion was thrown into harsh relief by the moonlight, and every object was clearly visible. But the ends and corners were in deep gloom, and the dull, distorted shadows of furniture were thrown up in weird patterns on the walls. All around me Maurice's ancestors glared down at me from their gilt-edged picture frames.

Forcing myself to remain calm, I put the candlestick down on a sideboard and padded across the drawing room with all the stealth of a burglar. That, at least, made me smile to myself. I picked up a handful of magazines—then froze in sudden panic. Behind me, from the direction of one of the large casement windows, I heard a dull, but definite scratching sound. My heart started to pound in fright as my imagination ran wild. Someone was trying to get in!

Chapter 5

For what seemed like an eternity I stood frozen to the spot, hardly daring to breathe as I strained to hear the slightest sound. Then, as everything remained eerily silent, I slowly turned, fully expecting at any second to be grabbed by some unknown assailant. I nearly laughed out loud with relief at what I found.

Obviously the catch on one of the casements had been loose, for the window now stood partially open and a gentle breeze billowed the drapes slightly. Perhaps a little extra gust had been enough to shake the latch loose. I didn't know, but that was no doubt the source of the noise I'd heard. At any rate, there was certainly no one besides myself standing in the room.

Breathing a little more easily now, I put the magazines down on a nearby table and walked over the window. As I reached it I heard another, more familiar sound—the muffled purr of a motor. *Probably just that fellow Tony returning from Perigueux,* I thought, as I peered outside.

What I saw, to my surprise, was the shadowy bulk of a large car, its yellow fog lights glowing in the moonlight. Near the car something was moving, but all I could make out were a couple of indistinct shadows.

I still hadn't realized what was going on when I was

startled by another shadow as it detached itself from the wall beside the window out of which I was staring, and dashed off across the terrace at top speed. One of the other shadows took off in pursuit, while its companion remained near the car. The fleeing shadow put on a burst of speed and disappeared under the cover of the trees.

For a moment, I simply remained where I was, staring out of the window in disbelief. Then, as the pursuing shadow returned toward the car, I instinctively reached out and closed the window as quietly as I could.

Panic was beginning to build within me now. I had no idea what was going on, but I certainly didn't want to be discovered in the drawing room at this late hour, an unwilling witness to a scene that bore all the earmarks of something unpleasant. Whoever was out there might very well think I was spying, and the consequences could be very nasty indeed. Forgetting both the candle and my magazines in my haste, I tore out of the room and dashed headlong up the stairs to my room.

Once I had regained my sanctuary I tried to collect my wits and calm the pounding of my heart. What, I wondered, could possibly be the meaning of all these strange comings and goings? I strained my ears to catch the slightest sound, but nothing happened. The silence was total.

My mind was a riot of conjectures. I wanted to know who had pursued whom, and why. And who, I wondered, could be the owner of the car that had appeared so stealthily in the middle of the night? Surely Alys had heard something and was aware of what had happened. And yet, there was no sound of movement from her room, located only a couple of doors down from my own. Then I remembered the bits of conversation I had overheard that afternoon; something about "later tonight." Had Alys expected something like this to happen?

The tall window of my bedroom looked out over the grounds, but in a different direction from those of the drawing room. I went over to take a look. All was quiet on this side: I couldn't detect any movement.

I was in a state of complete turmoil. Since it was quite obvious that I was unable to forget the whole thing and go to bed, I stayed by the window, both hoping and fearing to see someone, to hear cries for help. I felt menaced by something that I couldn't identify. Delacour Manor seemed suddenly full of hidden danger, and I wondered what on earth I was doing there—for all I knew, right in the midst of it.

Seconds, minutes, ticked by . . . half an hour. I looked at my traveling alarm clock, which I'd placed on the bedside table. I was surprised to see that it was only a little past eleven o'clock.

It wasn't all that late, I realized. Elsewhere, people were still up, going about their ordinary evening activities. But here we were shrouded in the depths of the forest, surrounded by a silence that was positively sepulchral.

I stayed on the lookout for a few more minutes, then went over and cautiously opened my door a crack. The silence remained unbroken, a cloying, suffocating silence.

This is ridiculous, I thought. *Here I am, creeping around like a common thief when I'm supposed to be a houseguest!* I decided to go find out what was happening. I certainly couldn't remain in my room, given my present state of nerves, waiting for the dawn to relieve my anxiety.

Taking a deep breath, I stepped out into the hall and walked firmly down the stairs and into the drawing room. Except for my candle, which had long since died out, it was as I'd left it. I hurried over to the window and looked out: all was calm, unmoving, normal. The car with the yellow fog lights had disappeared. Picking up the magazines and the candlestick I wandered slowly back to my room, deep in thought.

WHEN I ENTERED the dining room the next morning, I was greeted by an attractive sight—crusty homemade bread, golden pancakes with a touch of honey, rolls of butter and translucent marmalade.

It was still early, around eight o'clock. But I'd wanted to get up early to organize my departure.

As Alys suddenly appeared through a door that I assumed led to the kitchen, the sounds and smells of breakfast cooking came my way. She was carrying a pot of fragrant, steaming coffee on a silver tray. With a kick of her heel, she closed the door behind her and walked across the room.

"Good morning," she said in a friendly enough fashion. "I hope you don't mind having breakfast in the dining room. Lucy's handicapped by her age as well as her rheumatism, and I can't ask her to take trays up to the rooms."

I assured her that I was very happy to have breakfast in the dining room. "By the way," I added, hoping to sound casual, "it was a pretty eventful night last night, wasn't it?"

Her eyes widened as she looked at me in astonishment. "Eventful?" she echoed. "You didn't sleep well?"

"Not really," I replied. "In fact, I didn't get to sleep much before dawn. What with the incident in the courtyard and everything, I had quite a bit of trouble getting to sleep."

She gave me a puzzled look. I wondered whether she was going to tell me she didn't know anything about it and that I must have been seeing things. If she was acting, she certainly had talent.

"I'm talking about a scuffle—" I began.

"A scuffle, in the courtyard?" she interrupted, knitting her brown in concentration.

"Well," I persisted, determined to get to the bottom of the story, "I really did see a car and a couple of men. They were chasing another man."

"Oh," she said, with a slight wave of her hand. "Last night . . . ." Her casual gesture suggested that it was a matter of no great importance.

"It happened a little before midnight," I added, in case she needed further clarification.

"Ah, yes," she conceded, as she poured me out a cup of the delicious-smelling coffee. "I thought I heard something going on out there. It must have been around eleven-thirty. Do you take milk?"

"Yes, thanks."

She buttered some slices of bread and offered me one. "Lucy could have toasted this bread," she said apologetically.

I preferred it plain, but having no desire to encourage this attempt to change the subject, said nothing to reassure her. Of course, she would have had every right to claim that all this was none of my business, but my curiosity was now thoroughly aroused and I'd been too affected by what had happened to go along with her efforts to steer the conversation in another direction.

Innocently I asked, "Was he found?"

"Who?"

"The man—the fugitive. I saw him take off in that direction." I pointed through the open casement window at the wood.

"I don't know anything about it," she said. "I haven't spoken to anyone concerned."

I looked at her in complete amazement. "What!" I exclaimed. "Strangers come trespassing on your property in the middle of the night and you're not the slightest bit worried about it? Shouldn't you at least contact the police?"

My cry of disbelief had been entirely involuntary and my tone of voice must have been a little sharp, for she suddenly raised her head to look at me. Her eyes met

mine in a long, calculating stare. Then she twisted her
hands in a gesture of irritation. "I can guess what it was
all about," she said slowly, "and there isn't any need to
bother with the police, I assure you. But I'm sorry that
your sleep was disrupted. I would have warned you
about it before you went to bed last night if I'd realized
you were going to be disturbed."

I said nothing. She must have sensed that I was upset
by what had happened and wouldn't be satisfied with
this halfhearted explanation, for she sighed and then
added, "There's a private mental hospital not far from
here. One of the patients managed to elude the attendants and ran away. That was what that visit yesterday
afternoon was about. Some people from the hospital
came to ask me if I'd seen him. They were looking for
him in this neighborhood. The car that came here last
night must have been from the clinic. I suppose the two
people you saw were male nurses who'd been ordered
to bring their patient back again.

"There's no need to be alarmed," Alys said soothingly,
noting what must have been a look of sheer amazement
on my face. "None of the patients is dangerous. This
isn't the first time that one of them has escaped." With a
shrug she added, "They always catch them. Or their
family brings them back if they've managed to find their
way home."

Before I could say anything, she changed the subject
abruptly. "By the way, Tony's ready to help you, but
he's in a bit of a hurry. Do you want to see him?"

"Of course, right away," I said, focusing my attention
for the time being on my more immediate concerns. I
would have time later to think about Alys's explanation
of the previous night's activities.

Alys rang a bell and Lucy appeared at the door. At
her mistress's request, she fetched her son, a swarthy,
raw-boned youth who reminded me of his mother. He

seemed shy in the presence of a stranger and he didn't
venture to raise his eyes to look at me.

"Is your motorcycle ready?" Alys asked curtly.

"Yes, ma'am," Tony replied.

"Miss Charbonneau would like you to do something
for her. You're to take your motorcycle and go into
Neuvic, to the car-rental agency. Tell them to send
someone to fix the car. But don't dawdle on the way.
When are you going to work?"

"This afternoon. I'm on the three o'clock shift."

"That's good. You'll have plenty of time to go to
Neuvic and back." Alys explained that Tony worked in
a shoe factory a few miles down the river.

Not wanting to cause any unnecessary trouble, I said,
"All Tony has to do is telephone my agency in
Périgueux. They'll bring me another car."

"That's right, I forgot!" Alys exclaimed. "Your agency
is in Périgueux. Well, Tony, you'd better get going right
away. We don't want Miss Charbonneau to be detained
any longer than is absolutely necessary."

Then turning to me she added, "The driver certainly
won't get here before late morning. It's about twenty-
five miles from here to Périgueux and these agencies are
never in much of a hurry."

I asked Tony to be sure to tell the rental agent just
how annoyed I was for all the trouble his defective car
had caused me. When the lad had gone I turned to my
hostess. "If you don't mind," I said to her, "I'd like to
take a stroll around the grounds and perhaps a bit into
the forest while I'm waiting for them to come and bring
me another car."

As I'd suspected, Alys was delighted by my
suggestion. I knew that she hadn't been looking forward
to keeping me company. "That's a splendid idea," she
said, almost warmly. "I hope you won't mind if I don't
accompany you. I'm going away this afternoon, and I'll
be gone for a month or two, so I really have a lot of

packing to do. You have a good two to two and a half hours ahead of you. Try not to get lost!"

Alys was going away . . . for a month or two! Odd that she didn't mention it before, I thought. But then maybe she just decided to get away from the memories of the house. My sudden arrival and talk about Maurice must have upset her terribly. She was probably going back to her friends in Paris. . . .

I put on my coat, picked up my trusty camera and went out the door. I walked around the manor house, then started down the driveway with no particular destination in mind. It was a beautiful, sunny day, and as I walked along I gratefully drew in lungfuls of fresh air. I was delighted to have escaped the inhospitable atmosphere of the house itself.

As I reached the end of the long, tree-lined driveway and turned onto the narrow forest road that I'd driven over the day before, I suddenly remembered the gray ruins I'd glimpsed on my way in to Delacour Manor. I reckoned they couldn't be very far from where I was.

I decided to go visit them and take some pictures. I walked along the forest road, retracing the route I'd traveled in the now defunct Renault, and soon came to the rough dirt road that branched off toward the so-called Abbot's House. Expecting to reach the ruins in a few minutes, I hurried along the rough track, which was obviously little used. To my surprise, my goal was farther away than I thought, and it was a good half hour before the crumbling towers of an ancient fortress abbey emerged from the dense forest.

Much of the abbey was in complete ruin, but part of the main body of the building was still standing, flanked by a turret and a stone staircase that led to a cloister with Gothic arches, adjoining a small chapel. I admired the slender, graceful columns of the half-ruined gallery, smothered in dark, dense ivy.

The tower, I was sure, would be dangerous to explore.

Most of the buttresses seemed to have collapsed, and I was afraid that the ancient stones would crumble away from beneath my feet. Discretion being the better part of valor, I decided against climbing it.

The shadows were so deep around the ruins that I had little hope of getting some good pictures. I did, however, manage to photograph a beautifully carved bay window that had been momentarily illuminated by a ray of sunshine. I promised myself that I'd visit the abbey again someday at high noon, when the sun would be strong enough to pierce the curtain of vegetation. *Someday*, I thought, *when I've got plenty of time.*

As I was about to clamber up on the pile of rubble where I'd sat for moment to look the place over, I heard a faint noise coming from the ruins. Some stones came loose and rolled down the steps of the staircase. "Hello there," I called out, my curiosity aroused.

The noise stopped.

"Is someone up there?"

The heavy silence continued all around me, punctuated now and then only by the shrill, grating cries of the huge black crows that haunted the ruins in large numbers. From time to time, one of them lumbered forward and lunged into flight. *It must have been a crow*, I thought. One of them had probably dislodged the stones that had startled me.

Nevertheless, for some reason I suddenly felt decidedly uneasy. All at once, I wanted to turn around and run. Ashamed of my faintheartedness, I fought down this absurd desire. Picking my way amid heaps of rubble, I moved off in the direction of the chapel, and as I did so, I was amazed to catch a glimpse of some frescoes through a gaping arch. They had been badly faded by the sun.

It took me several minutes of careful looking before I found a place to slip through into the interior. But as I stepped onto the floor of the chapel, I stopped dead in my tracks, overcome with astonishment.

Chapter 6

A man was hard at work on a mural painting. He was standing on a makeshift platform, and although he couldn't have failed to hear me come in and leap down onto the tiles of the floor, he never even spared a glance in my direction.

"Oh . . . excuse me," I stammered in confusion.

He didn't turn around, seemingly too busy to interrupt his task. "At least let me finish," he growled. His voice, though unfriendly, was that of a cultured man. Suddenly I didn't feel nervous anymore. In fact, I began to feel decidedly annoyed.

"Oh, don't disturb yourself on my account," I remarked casually.

He needed no reassurance and carried on with his painting, totally absorbed in his work, as if I wasn't there.

My pride was stung and my anger and embarrassment were increasing by the minute. I felt like leaving but couldn't immediately see an exit. Besides, I wanted to have a better look at this artist, whom at present I could only see from the back.

Gingerly I took a few steps forward and pretended to

study a delicate pattern of tracery that had been carved in the ancient stone of a partition wall. But the depressing silence and the oddness of the situation finally got to me. Hesitantly I attempted to start a conversation. "I didn't know there was anyone up here," I said.

"Just me and the crows," he replied curtly. However, he did at least turn around to look down at me from his high perch. I noticed that his eyes had the same gray color as the slate tiles that covered the abbey's roof and turrets. And they were equally devoid of expression.

Nevertheless, there was a hint of liveliness in his appearance, and his angular, somewhat arrogant face was deeply tanned. He wore blue jeans and an open-necked shirt, revealing a bronzed throat and part of a muscular chest. In front of me was no callow youth: there was a manly cast to his features and a mature, surprisingly determined set to his mouth.

For several minutes we studied one another in silence. As he continued to stare at me, I began to find something stubborn, even hostile, in the square cut of his jaw.

I smiled at him shyly, but he didn't respond to my tacit offer of friendship. However he did break the silence. "What are you doing here?" he asked abruptly. "And who are you, anyway?"

His tone was cold and impersonal, almost disdainful, and I wondered cynically if this type of reception was typical of the people in this part of the country. On the other hand, I had to admit that he had a right to be suspicious of my unexpected intrusion into his domain. I hastened to explain the reason for my presence. "I'm a tourist," I told him, "and this is my first visit to the area. I was out for a walk and these old ruins intrigued me."

"What in God's name would a tourist be doing in this deserted spot?" he asked in disbelief.

"I'm just having a look around," I replied. "The scenery is worth it."

"There are plenty of other old ruins around here," he pointed out. "Why pick on this one? Quite apart from anything else, it's dangerous. It's half falling down and you can get hurt climbing around in here."

He came down off his perch and gathered up his materials. Then he straightened and looked me over, his gray eyes seemingly roving from the tips of my toes to the top of my head in a long, lazy insolent stare. Highly embarrassed and becoming more and more angry, it took every ounce of my willpower to meet his steady gaze.

"And I thought for sure I'd have the place to myself," he remarked finally and with what sounded like bitterness. "Even here, no one will leave me in peace."

"Well, you won't have to worry about me again," I retorted sharply, by now thoroughly annoyed. "Being insulted isn't on my list of enjoyable pastimes. I'll be leaving as soon as I can find my way out of here."

I looked around hurriedly, but try as I might, I couldn't find a breach in the wall through which to get out. He observed my futile efforts for a few minutes, an ironic smile on his lips.

After a while he shrugged, obviously convinced that my attempts to find a way out weren't sincere. "Visitors!" he snorted derisively. "No matter where you go, you can't get away from their prying."

His unconcealed rudeness brought a flush of real anger to my cheeks.

"Are you alone?" he asked abruptly.

"Naturally," I retorted. "Do you think I came with a whole busload of people? I'm afraid I'm not much one for group tours."

"Well that's something, at least," he remarked calmly, never even batting an eyelid at the sharpness of my reply. He continued to study me, like a botanist who'd just come across an unusual species of plant. "You're not afraid?" he inquired finally.

"Of what?" I asked, feigning surprise, for I knew exactly what he meant.

"Of me."

"Not at all," I replied airily, uncomfortably aware that I wasn't being entirely truthful. In fact, this initial exchange had left me feeling quite uneasy, but I certainly wasn't about to give him the satisfaction of hearing me admit it. "You don't look at all like the dangerous type to me," I added, just to make sure the message reached home.

"Well, you never know," he said, and I was sure I saw a faint smile cross his lips. For a moment we confronted one another in silence, like two adversaries measuring each other's strength. It took a considerable effort on my part to maintain a calm exterior, but at last I thought I saw the hard set of his features relax just a little.

"Well, I must say," he declared in a lighter tone, "it's a bit reckless of you to venture into the bear's cave like this."

"The only bear I've noticed around here is you," I retorted caustically.

Now I *did* see a smile—albeit a ghost of one, and quickly repressed—crease the corners of his mouth. "Touché," he murmured softly.

"Do you always greet your visitors this way?" I queried, only partially mollified. "Or am I just a special case?"

"Oh, you're nothing special, I assure you," he replied cheerfully.

I searched my mind for a suitably cutting retort, but failed to find one. All I could do was stand there, fuming silently, while he continued to stare at me, a gleam of amusement in his eyes.

Then his face softened somewhat as he said quietly,

"However, it isn't often that I receive such an attractive visitor. I don't suppose the original Goldilocks was half as pretty. I apologize for my boorish behavior." And with a little flourish he gave a low, formal bow.

"I accept the apology," I replied with a grin, then burst into laughter. Despite my initial aversion to this insolent, outspoken artist, I had to admit there was something rather appealing about him. For a start, he was extremely good-looking, though not in any conventional sense. He was, if anything, the picture of the Bohemian artist—shaggy and unkempt. His mop of thick dark hair was clean and shiny, but looked as though it saw a comb only once a day. It framed a dark-complexioned face with wide-spread eyes and fine, aristocratic-looking features, but there was the suggestion of strength and determination in the straight line of the mouth. His hands, I noticed, had the long, slender fingers of an artist. I judged him to be about thirty and well over six feet in height, and although he was lean, his physique was that of a well-conditioned athlete—broad shouldered and powerful.

But there was something else about him that appealed to me, although I couldn't quite put my finger on it. Perhaps it was the crease at the corner of his mouth; or the complete lack of "manners," combined with an ability to turn on the charm, as he had just then, whenever the occasion warranted. Or perhaps it was his way of looking at me, curious and observant, as if he were trying to guess what I thought of him.

In fact, he was looking at me like that now, as I finally managed to stop laughing. "I'm sorry," I spluttered. "I didn't mean to be rude. It's just that . . . . I stopped, unsure of how to continue.

"I'm delighted that you should find my apology so amusing," he remarked dryly.

In an effort to change the subject before we got back

onto dangerous ground, I said, "It just struck me as
rather funny that people in France know the story of
'Goldilocks and the Three Bears' as well as we do."

"Oh, so you're not French?"

"No, I'm from Canada. I'm just over here for a visit."

Suddenly he seemed interested. "So you're Canadian,"
he said. "From Montreal?"

"Yes."

This new information seemed to bring about a change
in his attitude. He didn't exactly relax completely, but at
least he wasn't on the defensive any longer. In some
ways, he reminded me of a duelist who, learning that he
has a poor opponent, drops his guard somewhat. Obviously the fact that I was a foreigner from afar, who'd
suddenly appeared and would probably disappear just as
quickly, had reassured him. "A Canadian," he repeated
thoughtfully. "How in heaven's name did you wind up
here?"

"I'll tell you about it one of these days, if you'll allow
me to visit your delightful old home." I don't know
what made me say it. The words just seemed to pop out
of my mouth of their own accord. Certainly after his
unfriendly reception, a return visit should have been the
last thing on my mind, but suddenly I knew I wanted to
come back—very much indeed.

"My home?" he queried.

"The Abbot's House. What a romantic name! I mean,
presumably you *do* live here? Are you on a retreat?"

The light in his eyes suddenly died and his face took
on a hard, bitter expression. "A retreat," he murmured.
"You don't know how right you are."

Obviously my comment had sparked the memory of
something unpleasant in his life, but he didn't elaborate.
Well, I thought, *let him keep his secrets*. I didn't want to
pry.

An instant later, with an abrupt change of tone and

expression, he asked lightly, "So you like ruins, do you?"

"Yes, I do," I replied. "The ones in this area have so much character, I can't help being attracted to them."

He seemed to approve my sentiments, but a shadow of suspicion flickered in his gray eyes. "You really like this countryside?" he persisted. "You're sure it's not just snobbery on your part?"

"Snobbery? Of course not," I replied indignantly. "I only arrived here yesterday and already I love the place."

He nodded approvingly, obviously sharing my enthusiasm for this part of France. "In that case," he declared, "I owe you an explanation of my remark." He shook his head in a gesture of disapproval. "Unfortunately, it's become very fashionable to have a country home in this area. People from Paris are buying up all the old ruins around here just to be able to say, 'We've got an adorable old place down in the Périgord. Do come down and visit us sometime.' " His affected imitation of the gestures and accent of well-to-do socialites made me laugh in appreciation.

"They really make me sick," he added vehemently, and in a gesture of disgust swung his paintbrush through the air, accidentally splattering some paint on my face.

Immediately his anger was forgotten in his concern for me. He sprang forward, a spotless white handkerchief appearing from nowhere in his hand. "Oh, Lord! Now look what I've done!" he exclaimed. "Forgive me, please. I really am treating you rather badly, aren't I?"

"Don't worry," I laughed. "My face is wash and wear, I assure you."

He gave me a quick grin, then cupped my chin in his left hand while with his right hand he began very gently to wipe off the paint. The sudden cool touch of his long sensual fingers acted like an electric shock to my system and set every nerve end tingling. Not daring to meet those cool, gray eyes so close to my own, I held my breath as he carefully and painstakingly completed the job.

When he'd finished, his left hand remained where it was for a minute, and I could feel his eyes boring into me as he gazed down at me. Then he stepped back and surveyed his handiwork. "Hmm—I don't know," he remarked thoughtfully. "I think I preferred it with green splotches." He gave a quick grin and added, "No, really, I am sorry."

"Please don't apologize," I said quickly, still a little breathless from the shock of his touch. "It's my fault. After all, I invaded your territory, and you don't seem to care very much for visitors."

"Well, I didn't realize you were Canadian," he said. "I'd have been more hospitable if I'd known. I certainly don't want you going away with a bad impression of the Périgord. Where are you staying, by the way?"

I told him that I'd rented a little house beside the river, not far away. "In fact," I added, "I ought to be going now. I have to move in there today." I looked at my watch.

"You're planning to walk there?" he asked, and waited attentively for my reply. He glanced around the ruins for the abbey, as if expecting someone to arrive.

"No," I replied. "Someone's going to pick me up shortly."

"Here?" he queried sharply. The idea that yet another visitor might invade his private domain obviously didn't appeal to him in the slightest.

I hastened to reassure him. "No, not here. You won't be bothered by anyone else."

"Well, that's a relief," he commented, then added superfluously, "I believe you are passingly familiar with my reaction to visitors."

"The thought had certainly crossed my mind," I

conceded with a smile. Then I told him about my misadventure with the Renault and explained that someone was coming from the rental agency to bring me another car. He didn't press me for details.

I summoned my courage to ask, "Would you mind if I came back here again?" Anxiously I waited for his reply. My curiosity had been awakened by this handsome artist and I wanted to learn more about him. Then, too, I didn't know anyone in the neighborhood and felt that it would be pleasant to have at least one friend to whom I could talk when the feeling arose.

"You want to visit the Abbot's House?" he queried after a moment. Then he shrugged. "I don't see why not."

"Thank you. You do me a great honor."

"But make sure you don't bring anyone with you," he added in a warning tone. I could read in his face that he meant exactly what he said.

"You like being all alone up here?" I ventured timidly.

"Most definitely," he declared firmly, his voice tinged with hostility. "I have absolutely no desire to be surrounded by people, believe me."

I wondered what he'd suffered to make him so jealous of his privacy. His gray eyes dimmed somewhat, and his mouth took on a bitter line. What was he doing, alone in this ruined abbey, cut off from the world like a monk in his cloister?

I thought of Alys, alone in her manor house. How strange, I thought, that they should be neighbors in this remotest of places, and yet they seemed to have nothing to do with one another.

"Don't worry," I said softly, "I won't bring anyone with me."

"In that case, you can come back." He gave a tight smile, but his eyes remained grim and the hard expression didn't leave his face.

I was about to say goodbye to him and ask him how

to find my way out of the chapel, but as I took one last look around, my eyes fell on the painting he'd been working on when I'd arrived. He was redoing the chapel frescoes. I couldn't help admiring the skillful way in which he'd applied fresh color to bring the ancient stones back to life.

He followed my gaze. "You like it?" he asked.

"It's marvelous," I murmured. "You've managed to recapture all the movement of the original."

He was obviously pleased at my compliment. Inclining his head, he stared critically at his handiwork. "Mmm, I must admit that painting is one of my stronger points," he conceded. "Do you like art?"

"I don't really know much about it," I confessed, "but yes, I do enjoy it. I've always been a bit envious of people who have the ability to express their feelings that way."

"Oh, well, in that case I can keep you jealous for hours," he remarked cheerfully. "I've got a whole studio full of the stuff. I'll have to take you up there and show it to you next time you come."

"I'd love to see it," I told him sincerely, delighted that he'd finally extended the invitation that, unconciously, I'd been hoping for.

It was getting late, I suddenly realized. "Well, I really must be going. Goodbye for now. Perhaps I'll see you soon."

He inclined his head in acknowledgement. "Take care on your way out of here," he warned.

For a moment he took my hand in his, and again his touch send a disconcerting tingling sensation through me. As he released his hold I turned, and without a backward glance almost ran from the ruins. Scrambling over the rubble, I heard him call out after me, "I'll be seeing you, Goldilocks." There was a hint of amusement in his voice, and I wondered what made him so sure of himself.

Chapter 7

Safely ensconced in my bed in the lock keeper's house, I was dreaming that I was dressed in a long, medieval gown, dancing in the arms of a tall man whose face I couldn't see. A noise suddenly awakened me: someone was banging loudly on the door. I got out of bed, put on my slippers and dressing gown, and hurried down the stairs to open the front door.

The woman standing outside introduced herself. "I'm Emma, ma'am. The real estate agent sent me over." Emma, who'd come to help me with the housework, was a sturdy country woman with red cheeks and bright blue eyes that twinkled merrily. I liked her immediately.

"And I'm Dawn," I replied warmly. "Please come in, Emma."

She gave me a pleasant smile as she bustled in. "They told me you were a nice young lady," she said, "and I can see that they were right."

I was delighted by this vote of confidence. *At last*, I thought, *I've met someone I can get along with from the start*. "That's your son outside?" I asked, seeing a young boy of about twelve standing in the boat tied alongside the little island.

"That's Patrick, all right. He's as curious as a cat. He's

been waiting to see the lady who's rented the lock keeper's house." She called through the doorway, "Hey, Patrick, come over and say hello to the young lady."

The boy climbed out of the boat and walked along the floating bridge to the house. When he got to the door he put out his hand to shake mine in typically French fashion.

"Hello," he said with a smile. "I'm Patrick."

"How do you do, Patrick," I returned. "My name's Dawn. I thought that boat belonged to the people who live in the château," I added, curious.

"It does, but they lend it to me," he replied nonchalantly. "My mom helps out with the cooking when they're there, and my dad looks after their cows and horses. So . . . ." he gave a slight shrug.

"So you have permission to use the boat? You're very lucky."

"Do you want to come with me for a little tour on the river?" Patrick asked. He seemed eager to make friends.

"Sure, I'd love to," I told him. "Just let me have a quick breakfast and then you can show me the sights."

A short time later, I climbed into the little skiff, which bore the rather grandiose name of *Salamander*. Patrick settled me down in the stern seat, untied the boat and pushed off from the landing dock.

As he rowed me along, I asked, "Where are you taking me, by the way?"

"Down the river. We can go as far as the dam. It'll only take half an hour. Okay?"

"Anything you say, skipper," I replied, giving him a smart salute and a grin.

"What do you want to do when you grow up?" I asked Patrick after a few minutes of companionable silence.

"I want to work at the Château Donazac, like my dad. I want to be manager of the estate. My Uncle George is the manager now. He looks after the tobacco,

the orchards, the rosebushes—everything. He buys all
the horses, and he even helps the cows when they're
calving. I help him out lots of times," he added proudly.

"You get along well with the Donazacs?"

"Oh, yes, they're really nice," he replied, his eyes
shining with genuine enthusiasm. "I like it when they all
come down to the château, because there are lots of
people around. There are all kinds of beautiful ladies, all
dressed up. They drive big cars and they like to play
tennis. And I like to play with my friends—Helen,
Sophie, Peter, Richard. . . ."

"They're the children?"

"Well, the younger ones, they're around my age.
There are lots of kids over there. We have parties, go
bicycle riding in the forest, rowing on the river, all kinds
of things. It's lots of fun. And their mothers always
invite me to stay and have lunch or supper."

"When do they arrive?" I asked.

"Sometime in the next few days."

I was excited at the prospect that there would soon be
some active social life in the neighborhood after all. I
thought of Alys, living in the depths of solitude like
Sleeping Beauty in her castle, and wondered why she
wasn't interested in cultivating the friendship of people
like the Donazacs. There seemed to be plenty of summer
residents who were out to enjoy themselves and surely
there was no need for her to live such a cloistered
existence. The fact that she was still in mourning didn't
explain everything.

"Patrick," I asked, "do you know an old manor house
called Delacour, not far from here?"

He nodded. "Sure, I know it." He gave me a wary
look, and I had the impression that my question had
embarrassed him.

I saw a flash of silver in the transparent water.
Suddenly my young companion bent over and grabbed a
carp that was swimming by. He moved so swiftly that I

was filled with admiration. "I've never seen anyone move so quickly!" I exclaimed.

"I've been fishing since I was six," he said proudly, dropping his catch in the bottom of the boat, from where it stared up at us with a baleful eye.

As we rowed to the dam and back, he chattered to me about various adventures he'd had with his Uncle George, his father and his summer friends at Château Donazac. When we returned to the landing dock, I thanked him for a delightful tour, and watched while he rowed off across the river in the direction of the château.

As I walked back to the house, I realized that I was still puzzled by Patrick's obvious reluctance to talk about Delacour Manor. I found Emma busy making lunch in the kitchen and decided to pursue my inquiry with her.

"Delacour Manor?" she said. "Sure, everyone around here knows it. . . ." Her voice trailed off. She seemed no more willing to discuss the subject than her son.

She looked down at the carrots she was peeling. I waited. Finally she whispered, "Ever since those stories got around. . . ."

I barely heard her, she'd spoken so low. "Stories? What stories?" I asked, my curiosity growing.

"About the accident. The man of the château is dead," she said, still looking down at her work.

"You mean Mr. Briançon? Mr. Briançon died in an accident?"

"That's what they say. . . ." I wondered what she meant to imply by this vague remark.

"What kind of accident?" I persisted.

"Something about a ladder. Nobody knows for sure. There's just rumors." This conversation was obviously making her uneasy.

"Rumors?" I echoed. I knew she didn't want to talk about it, but I pressed on, anyway. I'd already sent a telegram, rather than the letter I'd planned, to Norman about Maurice's death, but I would have liked to be able to tell him the whole story. "Emma, please tell me more about it."

But she froze. "It's none of my business, people talk . . . . But when you need work, it's better not to pay any attention to gossip."

"What sort of talk?" I prodded tenaciously.

"Bah! People . . . ." She shrugged, then got up and went over to put the carrot peelings into the garbage. "They say she wants to sell," she muttered, as she put a saucepan on the stove.

"She?"

"The widow, of course!" Emma spat out the word like an insult. Alys was obviously not one of her favorite people.

"And what does her neighbor have to say about that?" I asked. I threw in this last remark as casually as I could.

She raised her head and stared at me. I noticed that beneath her headscarf, her face had flushed beet red. "What neighbor?" she queried huffily.

"The one who lives in the Abbot's House," I replied.

"The Abbot's House? Nobody lives there. It's falling apart."

I was dumbfounded. "You must be joking," I protested. "I met the man who lives there."

"You're mistaken," she said emphatically, shaking her head. "You must have been somewhere else. The Abbot's House is an owl's nest: nobody's lived there for years."

"No, I was at the Abbot's House all right," I maintained. "It's just a couple of miles from Delacour. I saw a sign that identified it as the Abbot's House, and I even visited the chapel. There was a man there; he was busy. . . ."

I was going to say "painting," but I stopped myself

just in time, suddenly wary. *After all*, I thought, *this is none of my business. And if my artist doesn't want to let his presence be known, to avoid curious visitors, who am I to stand in his way?*

Luckily, Emma seemed to have concentrated on just one word I'd said: Delacour. She studied me, her face reflecting both surprise and disgust. "So you've been to Delacour?" she asked. "You know the lady there?"

She seemed suddenly suspicious of me, and I realized that she was probably wondering why I was asking her all these questions if I'd visited Delacour myself.

I wanted Emma to have a good opinion of me, and I didn't want to undermine the promising beginnings of our relationship. After all, if I was going to be staying in this house all summer, I'd better get along with her.

After a moment's reflection, I decided it would be best to tell her my story. At some length, I described the circumstances that had brought me to the Périgord, and the relationship that had existed between my family and Maurice Briançon.

As she listened her expression changed. "I understand now," she said with evident relief. "You must have been shocked to learn that the poor gentleman was dead."

I sighed in agreement. I was consumed with curiosity and was hoping that Emma would now loosen up enough to tell me more about the rumors concerning Maurice's death. But she said nothing more. She was, I realized, just the kind of stubborn countrywoman one meets the world over—suspicious of strangers, closemouthed and, at the slightest hint of a threat from outside, unquestioningly loyal to her own. I knew there was no point in pursuing the matter further.

Patrick came back, bringing the fish he'd caught.

"I'm going to make you a carp à la Neuvic," Emma announced as she went out to the courtyard to scale the fish.

The carp, stuffed with foie gras and truffles, was

delicious. I invited Patrick to stay with me to help me eat his fish and to keep me company.

He accepted my invitation without hesitation. After lunch was over, I went upstairs and rummaged around in my suitcase. I finally found the pendant I was looking for. It was, in fact, an Indian amulet, covered with mysterious signs of the Sioux tribe. I went downstairs and gave it to the young lad. My exotic present won him over completely and he promised to be my friend forever. "For life, for death," he intoned solemnly, spitting on the ground to impress me.

This grave ritual reminded me of my nephew Paul, Norman's son. *Kids*, I thought, *they're the same everywhere*.

I EMBARKED on my exploration of the Périgord with enthusiasm. I visited every corner of Périgueux, the fortified city of Domme and Brantôme, the hometown of Pierre de Bourdeille, the sixteenth-century adventurer who wrote biographies of famous men and women of his time, in imitation of the great classical author, Plutarch. For the next few days, I crisscrossed the area in my new Renault, took photos and piled up notes. I stopped at charming country inns, where I became thoroughly acquainted with the cooking of the Périgord: *clafoutis*, a kind of cherry tart; omelettes laced with savory truffles; foie gras by the spoonful; and the rich, creamy garlic soup that I welcomed everywhere. The wines, though not as famous as those of Bordeaux, were very acceptable and I enjoyed trying them.

Sometimes I plugged in my tape recorder in the kitchen and taped my conversations with Emma or with her husband, who occasionally came to do the gardening. Their language, as savory as their food, was a source of perpetual fascination for me; and as recorded on my cassettes, it would be one of the most delightful souvenirs of my stay in the Périgord.

A few days after my visit to the Abbot's House, I received a letter from Norman. He wrote to say that he was saddened by the news of Maurice's death, and he wanted to know any details I could find out. "Also, try to get a photo or a memento for me," he added. "Maurice's death seems to have erased a page from my youth. I'm deeply affected by it."

I suspected as much, for I knew that my brother was very sensitive. Much as I disliked the prospect, I decided to approach Alys as soon as she got back from her trip. It would have to be from her that I would obtain this last gift. I also intended to visit Maurice's grave—a gesture that Norman would appreciate, I knew—and its whereabouts would have to be obtained from his widow.

Added to that, of course, was the fact that I wanted to know how Maurice had died. The only information I'd been able to glean from Emma was that his untimely departure from this world was thought to have been caused by the accident. Other than that, speculation seemed rife throughout the neighborhood. Quite apart from my own curiosity, I wanted to be able to tell Norman the whole story, and hoped that perhaps another visit to Delacour would elicit more information from its coldly beautiful mistress.

Alys had only been gone two weeks at this point. I knew I'd have to wait another six weeks or so before calling on her. That didn't stop me speculating on the visit, though. And I was not optimistic. I didn't know quite why I felt this ill-defined hostility toward Alys. No doubt her initial cool reception and inhospitality had a great deal to do with it, but there was something more to it than that. Perhaps it was the way in which she'd deftly avoided answering some of my more probing questions concerning her husband's death. Whatever the reason, I knew I didn't trust her.

On impulse I decided to pay a visit to my artist

friend. It was, I realized, a bit presumptuous of me to think of this man as a friend, but as I knew so few people in the area I was eager to cultivate his company. And I had to admit, I was very curious about the hermit of the Abbot's House.

When I reached the road sign pointing to the ruined abbey, I realized that I was right and Emma had been wrong. I'd been certain that it had been the Abbot's House I'd visited, but it was reassuring to have my conviction confirmed.

I turned off onto the rough dirt road, and after a few minutes, pulled up near the ruins. As I was walking along the stony pathway leading up to the abbey, I met an old peasant woman. At least on first glance she appeared old. As I looked more closely at her face I saw that she was probably only fifty-five or sixty. A life of hard physical work had wrinkled her face cruelly; in spite of the wrinkles, though, there was an alertness to her that indicated to me she wasn't as old as I first thought. She had a muslin cape tied across her breast, and a black headscarf knotted tightly under her chin. She was wearing a black dress, like all the countrywomen of the Périgord I'd seen. I thought how much they reminded me of nuns.

The woman gave me a grim, suspicious look. She was carrying a woven wicker basket, which was also black, and seemed to be coming from the ruined abbey. When she came level with me, she stopped right in the middle of the track as though to bar my way. I gave her a smile of greeting, but she didn't brighten up at all. *They're really not very sociable around here*, I thought to myself wryly.

"This road doesn't go anywhere," she informed me in a harsh tone.

"But isn't this the way to the Abbot's House?"

She blinked, looking a little like a mole suddenly emerging into the bright light of the day. Glaring at me, she continued to block my passage along the narrow path. She muttered a few words that were unintelligible to me, then turned around and rushed off in the direction from which she'd come, as if the devil himself were pursuing her.

I stood there, dumbfounded. What, I wondered, had I said that was so extraordinary? And why had she turned and fled, instead of continuing on her way?

Chapter 8

For a few moments I stared after her in perplexity. Then, deciding that there was no point in attempting to understand the strange behavior of the locals, I continued on my way. Her black-clad figure had long disappeared into the ruins by the time I reached the chapel.

I called out in the direction of the staircase and the gallery. "Hello! Is anyone there?"

The crows cawed as they wheeled around over the pile of ancient stones. Behind one of the crumbling windows, under the gray slate tiles, I thought I saw something, or someone, move.

"Hello there, Mr. Bear! It's me, Goldilocks," I cried out at the top of my lungs. Ridiculous, I knew, but since I didn't know his name, what else was I to call him?

A face appeared, then disappeared. There were eyes spying on me, I knew: I could feel their presence like a tangible weight. A cautious voice came to me from high above. "Not so loud. You're alone?"

"Of course I am."

"Well, then, come on up . . . by the staircase. Watch out for the steps."

The warning was not superfluous, as I realized when I began to climb up the stairs. Loose stones rolled under my feet, and I stumbled several times before I reached the gallery.

The floor of the gallery was also strewn with rubble. As I moved on through the rooms of the ruined abbey, my surprise increased. What did it all mean, I wondered. Surely he couldn't be living here, where ghosts seemed to be the only possible inhabitants. The whole place had an abandoned look about it; there were no pieces of furniture, no trace of a human presence. The rain, the wind and the sun had become the masters of the Abbot's House.

Somewhat overcome by my impressions, I moved hesitantly forward through the remains of what had once been a monastery, with its chapter house, its ceremonial rooms, its reception halls and living quarters. I came across the remains of wonderful carved fireplaces that had been terribly mutilated by centuries of neglect and exposure to the elements. In many places, the beams of the high ceiling had fallen in.

I remembered that Emma had described the Abbot's House as uninhabitable, and realized that her remarks had not been far from the truth. I wondered how my friend, the artistic hermit, had managed to make a home for himself in the midst of these ancient ruins.

"Over here!" a voice from above called out encouragingly.

At the end of the last circular room, I saw a narrow, concealed staircase. I climbed up the stairs and emerged into an immense attic room.

My artist friend came over and stood next to me. "Walk carefully," he warned. "The floor is full of holes. Watch where you put your feet."

My heart began to beat a little faster, and I realized I was a bit nervous. Was it entirely due to the fact that I was afraid one of the floorboards beneath my feet would collapse at any moment? Or was it the knowledge that I was alone with this rather disconcerting man, whom I hardly knew, in a strange place?

"I can see you're not afraid of heights," I said with a smile, hoping he couldn't hear the slight tremor in my voice.

"Hello, Goldilocks." He held out his hand to guide me into his strange domain.

"Hello, Mr. Bear," I replied, gratefully accepting the proffered hand. "I thought you were one of the ghosts. There's something unreal about this place. It's quite an eagle's nest, isn't it?"

I looked around me in curiosity. I realized that we were in the upper part of the tower, under the slate tiles of the roof. Obviously this was where my host had established his living quartrs. His arrangements were very basic—an iron bed in a corner; a rickety table, which bore the remains of a meal; and stacks of bricks that served as primitive seats.

In a niche I noticed some canned goods, a stoneware pitcher, paper plates and a small water jug. There was a bowl of milk and a pot of honey on the table, and a pottery dish containing some half-rotten oranges and apples.

"What are you doing up here, in the midst of all this, ah, junk?" I exclaimed. I suppose, looking back, my comment was in fact quite rude.

"I paint," came the short reply.

"Well, I know that, but surely you could accomplish the same thing in more comfortable surroundings. What do you paint, anyway. Still life?"

"No, landscapes." He held out his strong, well-shaped hand to me once again. "Come and see. Don't be afraid. I may be a bear, but I won't eat you, I promise."

He pulled me toward a door that opened onto a circular balcony running around the tower, and I gave a gasp of astonished delight as I stepped outside. I was dazzled, fascinated, by the extraordinary vista that was spread out before me. All around us, far below, lay the dense forest, a thick, dappled carpet that seemed to be woven of every imaginable shade of green, with here and there a thread of gold running crookedly through it.

In the distance, across the valley and half-obscured in a bluish haze, I could see châteaus, villages and red-tiled houses scattered over the rolling hills in harmonious disorder. Their stone walls had a rosy tinge to them, as if imbued with sunlight. Far away on the horizon, the Isle River wound through the hills like a silver ribbon.

"What a breathtaking view," I murmured, though I knew the words were trite.

"It is rather lovely, isn't it?" he agreed softly. I sensed in his voice a deep pride, as if he were a magician who'd conjured up this fairyland for my special enjoyment.

"It certainly is," I replied fervently, still staring out over the magnificent countryside. "What an inspiration for an artist. No wonder you've chosen this place as a retreat."

He didn't answer me.

We stayed that way for a moment, to dream. I appreciated the fact that he was silent. This vision was beyond words. I drank it in with my eyes and heart: I was enchanted.

"I see you, also, feel its effect," he said quietly after a few moments. Then he added, "All of the dreams of my childhood are here, in this attic studio. This was where I began to paint, to communicate with nature, to watch the sunset blaze up on the horizon and then dissolve into it. This was where I learned to understand color and to acquire a passion for forms. In fact, I learned a whole new language, and for me, it was the real one."

Surprised at the sudden intensity in his voice, I tore myself away from my contemplation and turned to look at him. He was staring off into the distance, his eyes alight with a strange gleam, and I suddenly realized how badly I'd misjudged him. Up until now, I'd seen him as some sort of strange recluse shut in his own little world, shunning the company of others. And indeed, on the surface, this was exactly what he was. But now I had the impression that this was a front, a brick wall hiding a far more sensitive and passionate man behind its hard exterior. The unexpected vibrancy in his voice hinted at an enthusiasm for life that simmered only just below the surface.

I wondered who or what had caused his retreat from life when he was so obviously capable of enjoying it to the full. And noticing once again the strength and determination suggested by the square jaw and straight mouth, I also shivered slightly at the thought of what might happen if the passion that smoldered within him should explode in the wrong direction.

"Do you really live here alone all year round?" I ventured timidly.

He gave a slight, noncommittal shrug. "When they let me," was his strange reply. Almost breathlessly I waited for him to continue, hoping I might be about to learn something more about this strange man. I still didn't even know his name, much less anything else about him.

"They?" I prompted, when his silence threatened to lengthen into eternity.

But perhaps he felt he'd already said too much, for he simply gave a small frown of annoyance and remained silent. I didn't press him any further. After all, he knew as little about me as I knew about him, and I could hardly expect him to take me into his confidence right away. Still, I had to admit to a burning curiosity.

We had both become lost in our thoughts once more when a slight noise suddenly alerted us. I felt my companion's hand tighten on my wrist as he shot me a quick, warning glance. Then he turned, and crossing the balcony in swift, silent strides, entered the attic room. I followed in close, equally quiet pursuit.

A voice echoed in the stairwell and at once his face cleared. Throwing an "It's all right" over his shoulder to me, he went over to the staircase and spoke to whomever was arriving. A moment later the woman I'd met on the path appeared in the doorway. She and my host exchanged a few words in the local Périgord dialect, which I found almost impossible to understand.

The woman turned her head in my direction. A rapid, intense flow of words issued from her clenched teeth.

He shook his head vigorously, obviously trying to persuade her of something. I had no doubt they were talking about me. Finally she left the rom, making gestures in my direction that plainly conveyed her hostility toward me.

"What's the matter with her?" I asked. "I met her on the way up here and she turned and fled from me as though all the devils in hell were pursuing her."

"Nothing to worry about," he assured me. "That's just Sarah. She came to warn me someone was coming."

"Sarah?" I queried.

"Yes. For some reason I'll never understand, but for which I'm heartily thankful, she's devoted to me. She does my shopping and housekeeping."

The housework, I thought, wouldn't be much of a burden in this place. Once Sarah had made the bed and put a couple of fresh paper plates on the table, her labors would be pretty well over.

"She doesn't seem to like me," I remarked. "Why not?"

He shrugged off my comment. "She's afraid for me," he explained.

"What's she got to be afraid of? I wouldn't say I'm much of a threat, and you're not a child. Maybe she thinks I'm bothering you?"

"Possibly," he conceded, "but that's for me to decide, not her. Anyway, since you're here, allow me to give you the grand tour of my palace."

"Palace" was hardly the right word to describe the place, I decided, as we stumbled over the heaps of rubble in the tower. The ancient beams that supported the roof and the superstructure made me think of a ship at anchor . . . but ready to move on the first tide. It must be quite something, I thought, when the wind blew through all these chinks and narrow, glassless windows. And terribly cold, too.

I wondered why there were so many iron wires stretched from one beam to another, and my host explained that they had once been used for drying tobacco.

After we had completed our inspection of the tower, we went back out onto the circular balcony and sat down facing the horizon. We talked. I told him a bit about life in Canada, and he seemed to be interested in what I had to say. Then I asked him about the Périgord. My curiosity, I explained, was partly motivated by my interest in making some TV programs about the area, to give my fellow Canadians some idea of the riches it contained.

He seemed to be enjoying himself, but it was rather hard to tell really, for he seldom smiled at my remarks. Nevertheless, he was certainly an attentive listener.

"Do you want to see my paintings?" he asked abruptly during a lull in our conversation.

"I'd love to."

He disappeared into the tower and emerged a few minutes later carrying a bundle of canvases. He set them out in front of me in the full light of day, one by one. Interested, then charmed, I admired them sincerely. As far as I, a nonspecialist, could judge, everything he did was in a highly personal style. I took a particular fancy to the play of colors in his paintings of the local scenes. He had managed to capture the somewhat primitive charm of the Périgord landscape, where the primordial harshness may be mellowed, suddenly and unexpectedly, by the gentle curve of a river, the soft reflections on a

tile roof or the fluid pattern of smoke escaping from a
chimney.

He went away and came back with a guitar that he
had found somewhere in the depths of this enchanted,
tumbledown dwelling. As I continued to study the works
produced by his undeniable talent, he started to play, as
if I wasn't there, as if he'd forgotten my presence. Indeed, perhaps he had, for he seemed totally immersed in
the music and didn't glance at me once during his recital.
He played folk songs—haunting melodies they were—
and his expression relaxed. He looked much younger, as
if an invisible hand had smoothed away the years.

I was enchanted, scarcely able to believe the scene—
the astonishing landscape, the paintings, the plaintive
music, the strange man beside me and myself. I was
eager to prolong the moment, to remain exactly where I
was with my back against the warm stone.

But with a tremendous effort of will, I shook myself
out of my semitrance. "Mr. Bear," I said, "I'm being
very impolite. I'm burdening you with my presence. It
must be terribly late."

"So you want to leave?" he inquired flatly.

I heard myself say, "Nobody's waiting for me."

"Nor for me, either."

Silence fell, as if it wanted to drown our two
solitudes. It wove a soft web around us and brought us
mysteriously closer together. *What beautiful eyes he has,* I
thought. *But unfathomable like an abyss. Can they be
tender sometimes?*

My heart, flooded with sudden warmth, began to beat
a little faster. I smiled faintly, not daring to move,
projecting an outward calm that belied the tumultuous
current of emotion overwhelming me within.

I felt his eyes upon me and hesitantly, almost
reluctantly, I turned to look at him. He held me in a
hypnotic gaze I was powerless to resist. And then his arm
was around me, drawing me close. Submissive to his

will, I melted into his grasp, pressing myself against his lean, hard body. As if in a trance, I watched as he bent his dark head over mine, and now I could feel the feathery-light caress of his breath on my face. Nervously, excitedly, I waited for the inevitable. And when it finally came, it was with a force so compelling, it left me both breathless and helpless. His mouth crushed down on mine, bruising, demanding, and I yielded instantly to its insistent urgings.

And when he finally released me, I knew for sure that a certain contained violence lay beneath the coolly controlled exterior of my artist.

Chapter 9

Thereafter I returned almost every day to see the hermit of the Abbot's House. He agreed to do my portrait. "On condition," he added, "that you bring me a new canvas. My supply is running out."

It was little enough to pay for a work of art. "With pleasure," I agreed readily.

He gave me the address of the shop in Périgueux where I would be able to find the material. "I can't send Sarah," he said. "She doesn't know anything about art supplies."

"I'm not sure that I do, either," I commented doubtfully. "Why don't you come into Périgueux with me and help me pick out a good canvas?"

It was the wrong thing to say. For a moment he simply stared at me coldly, then, in a voice all the more chilling for its calmness, he said, "I do not want to leave this place—*ever*. Is that clearly understood?"

"Yes . . . yes, of course," I assured him hurriedly.

In fact, I didn't understand at all, but wisely I did not pursue the matter. I simply told myself that he had every right to live in isolation in the depths of the forest, if that was what he wanted. But I did find his behavior somewhat strange, and again, I wondered what had caused this retreat from the world at large.

Every time I came to the ancient abbey, I was both impressed and dismayed anew by its air of solitude and neglect. I wanted to turn and go. But then I'd glimpse him watching me, half-hidden behind the arched Gothic windows of his studio. I realized that he made a practice of following my every movement as I got out of the car and came toward him along the narrow, stony pathway that was almost hidden by a dense thicket of holm oaks. We seemed to be enacting a scene from some forbidden medieval romance.

He never greeted me or indicated in any way that he was glad to see me, but he was always there at the top of the stairs, with his arrogant air and the faintest of mocking smiles on his face. He seemed to be very much a part of his surroundings, solitary and aloof, with his casual clothes, his tanned skin and the faint smell of ferns and bracken that clung to him.

He would watch critically as I climbed up the crumbling staircase toward him, my offhand and somewhat stilted smile of greeting concealing my feelings of embarrassment. Gradually, though, I learned to climb up those tricky steps without dislodging too many pebbles, and I grew accustomed to the discordant cawing of the crows.

In spite of the many misgivings I had about the wisdom of my visits to the abbey, I enjoyed them more than anything else I did. I realized that I'd be feeling very much at loose ends if I didn't have these opportunities to talk to someone intelligent—someone who was deeply attached to his native Périgord and who could explain its charms to me in such a sensitive way.

I brought him cigarettes, which he always accepted with a brief, impersonal thank you. Sometimes I ran into Sarah in the attic studio, busy with her housekeeping. She invariably left when I came in, throwing a hostile look in my direction.

On one occasion, however, she seemed ready to talk to me. Instead of avoiding me, as usual, she came toward me, looking at me intently. Her mouth moved as if she wanted to confide in me. But then she suddenly turned her back on me and walked away, muttering something in the unintelligible dialect of the region.

My artist friend, who'd been standing off to one side of the studio, came over to me. His eyes fixed on Sarah's back as she disappeared down the stairs.

"She certainly doesn't care for me!" I remarked ruefully.

"She's not friendly," he admitted with a shrug. "She's a little like me: she doesn't like strangers invading her territory."

"Well, in that case, I'll leave right now," I replied, stung by his remark.

"Hey, not so fast," he laughed, grabbing me by the arm as I turned to leave. "Haven't you learned by now that *you're* not a stranger?"

He could be very persuasive when he wanted to be. And I didn't really want to give up my visits to the Abbot's House. "Don't you ever leave your eagle's nest?" I asked in an attempt to cover the awkwardness I suddenly felt.

"Yes. Every morning I go down to the river for a swim. Very early when you, no doubt, are still lazing away in bed. Sometimes I fish, too, and Sarah cooks anything I catch." It occurred to me that he was really playing the part of the noble savage to the hilt.

I remember very clearly the day that he started work on my portrait. He sat me down on a wooden crate, crossed my hands over my knees and told me to turn to show him my profile.

"Turn a bit to the right and lift your chin up," he said. "There. That's good. Can you hold the pose, little one?"

"I do have a name," I protested, irritated by this patronizing way of referring to me. I wasn't about to play the little country girl to his Prince Charming.

"I'm sure you do," he said, apparently unperturbed by my remark. "And what is it, this name of yours?"

"My name is Dawn," I replied a little crossly.

"Dawn," he mused, surveying me with his head tilted to one side, as if to determine whether or not he thought it suited me.

"That's what my friends call me," I said with some asperity.

"Well, then, so will I," he replied without further ado.

I looked at him in perplexity. Was he teasing me, I wondered, or was this a disguised declaration of friendship? In any case, he seemed content to call me by my real name.

"Goldilocks isn't really an appropriate name for me, anyway," I said. "I'm not at all like the girl in the story."

"Oh, but you are," he contradicted cheerfully. "Goldilocks was, after all, a blonde, and was incautious enough to venture into the forbidden forest. Isn't that what you've done?"

"Well, I have to admit that I'm curious by nature. It comes with my job."

"Curiosity is a dangerous flaw, Dawn," he intoned with mock solemnity. "Remember what it did to the cat?"

"I don't care," I retorted childishly. I knew I was spoiling for a fight.

But he didn't respond to my challenge. Silence enveloped us like a veil.

He worked silently at the sketching for a while, then said, "You can keep on talking, if you like. It doesn't bother me."

Taking advantage of his offer, I asked, "If I'm not going to keep on calling you Mr. Bear, what should I call you?"

"My real name is Brett."

"That's a romantic name."

"We're a romantic lot around here," he replied, in an offhand manner.

He stopped speaking and became absorbed in his task. He worked quickly. With a few strokes of a pencil, he'd soon sketched a surprising likeness of me. The shape of my mouth was there, and the way my eyes crinkled slightly when I laughed.

"Am I so pretty?" I asked hypocritically.

He examined me with a serious air, as if he was asking himself the same question. "Prettier," he declared at last. "I'll have to improve my sketch. I forgot the dimple in your cheek, and I didn't get the curve of your chin right. But I've captured the fine shape of your nose, your high cheekbones and the slightly oval shape of your eyes."

He'd come over to me and run his fingers tantalizingly over my features as he spoke. Once again, I felt the tingling sensation his touch always produced in me, and I backed away slightly.

As I sat still once more, allowing him to continue with the portrait, I thought again of the time he'd kissed me. The memory of it remained vivid and at times I felt myself longing for him to kiss me again. As I looked at him now out of the corner of my eye, I recognized this to be one of the times. . . . I could feel my skin grow hot, and desperately I began to think of something else so that I wouldn't give myself away by blushing.

I began to talk about Canada. Brett seemed to be quite interested in what the people and the country were like, and he was intrigued by the fact that many Canadians still felt quite an attachment to Europe, especially France.

"By the way," I said, "when I was young I met one of your neighbors, Maurice Briançon. He was a good friend of my brother Norman, and he came over to visit us in Montreal one summer. You know, the owner of Delacour Manor, the one who died recently. We were very sorry to hear about it. Norman loved him like a brother.

I was still posing, my head bent, offering my profile. A tense silence lengthened between us and I wondered if he'd really heard what I'd said.

"That's enough work for today," he said suddenly.

Surprised, I stretched and jumped to my feet as he pushed aside his easel with a weary gesture.

"May I look at it?" I asked.

"No. It's not finished." His mouth was tense. He packed away his equipment with quick, angry gestures. I didn't want to pry into the reason for his sudden fit of bad temper, and I got ready to go. He didn't hold me back, obviously wanting to be left alone again.

How mercurial he is, I thought. *His mood can change from one moment to the next, for no apparent reason.* I realized how very sensitive I had become to the mysterious currents of emotion that lay beneath his impassive outward appearance. I knew that at the moment, he couldn't bear to be in anyone's company, not even mine, and I wondered what I'd said to provoke such a sudden change.

WHEN THE PEOPLE who owned the Château Donazac arrived for their summer holidays, they brought a whole new life to the area. I took a great liking to them: their youth and liveliness were a welcome change from the somewhat excessive tranquillity of the neighborhood.

I watched from my little house across the water as the elegant Renaissance windows of the ivy-covered keep and turrets were thrown open. Now there was a continual bustle of people coming and going at the Gothic entrance porch of the château, which linked up to the bridge across the moat. Sports cars discharged young women in fresh summer clothes. From the direction of the tennis courts, I heard joyful cries of the players and the dull thud of balls striking rackets. A group of children took over the small boat, evidently deciding to make the river their home for the summer. They seemed to be a lively, good-natured bunch.

I soon made friends with the children, and it wasn't long before their mothers, Ann and Catherine, two sisters who looked almost like twins, came over to visit me. They seemed as eager to be neighborly as I was.

I was delighted. I had been feeling a bit lonely in my little house beside the water. Except for my visits to Brett's studio, I had very little to do when I'd finished my work or my exploration of the Périgord for the day.

I was quick to respond to the overtures of my neighbors. When they invited me to come over to have a cup of tea on their terrace, I accepted immediately.

The terrace of the Château Donazac was a beautiful spot overlooking the meandering banks of the green and tranquil waters of the river. The château itself was an elegant, medieval dwelling of splendid proportions, the architecture pure and balanced. The interior had been provided with all the modern conveniences and furnished in the best of taste. A true pleasure palace, I thought, and one to delight the heart of many a city dweller.

The Isle River seemed almost to have been placed there deliberately, to serve as a mirror for this architectural gem. I couldn't help admiring the great skill with which the architects of the period had been able to make their buildings harmonize so well with the landscape.

I promised myself to make use of every opportunity to come and relax in this atmosphere, and to cultivate the friendship of these charming people.

I ALMOST LOST the chance, for a few days later I very nearly came to grief, and even now, when I think of it, an involuntary shudder runs down my spine.

I'd awakened in my cozy little house as the first rays

of the morning sunshine were streaming through my windows. Preoccupied as I'd been with getting to know my new neighbors, I suddenly realized I hadn't been back to see Brett for three days. Our last parting had been rather cool and I imagined that he must be wondering what had happened to me.

I got dressed quickly. When I went down to the kitchen, I found that Emma had brought me some of her special cherry tarts, and a chicken pâté with truffles that was, according to the accompanying card, a gift from my new friends at Château Donazac. I decided to pack a picnic lunch and go visit the solitary artist.

It was early. As I glanced out the window, I saw that the château across the water was still bathed in the rosy glow of sunrise. I took down a wicker basket and began to fill it with good things for my picnic. I put in Emma's tarts and the chicken pâté, then added some fresh cheese I'd picked up at the market, some fruit and a bottle of local wine.

I drove off toward the forest in my little Renault. As I had foreseen, Brett wasn't expecting me at this early hour and had gone out for his usual swim. I set out my provisions on the studio table, then walked out onto the circular balcony and looked down to get my bearings. Once I was sure which way to go to reach the river, I went down the stairs and out of the abbey. I found the path leading to the river and rushed along it, hoping to surprise Brett. It was farther than I thought, and it took me quite a while to get there. I had to go down a narrow, badly marked trail, then cross a field and walk along the river bank. By this time, I was drenched with dew from the long grass.

For a moment, I thought I'd made a mistake: I couldn't locate the landmarks I'd seen from the tower. I was ready to give up on my little expedition and turned to go back to the abbey. At that very moment I caught sight of him on the other side of the river. He was packing up his fishing gear. I saw that his swimsuit was hung out on a branch to dry.

"Hello!" I called. "Have you had your swim already?"

He gave a sudden start and peered sharply over the river. Then he recognized me. "What are you doing here so early in the morning?" he called back across the water.

"I was tempted by the idea of going for a swim," I replied cheerfully. "Watch!"

I slipped out of my dress. I'd already put my swimsuit on underneath, before I left the house.

"The water's cold. You'd better not go in," he warned.

"It doesn't frighten me."

He cupped his hands and raised his voice. "What did you say?"

"I said that cold water doesn't frighten me. I'm used to it. I'm coming over to you." So saying, I took off my sandals and stepped to the edge of the river bank.

"Hey, not so fast!" he cried, a note of real alarm creeping into his voice. "At least wait until I show you the place to cross over."

But I paid no attention. After all, I couldn't see any reason to worry. The water was crystal clear and calm: I could have counted the little white pebbles that glistened on the bottom.

I dove into the water and started to swim toward him. But I soon ran into trouble; the current was a great deal stronger than it looked.

Brett watched me attentively from the far bank. I couldn't make out his expression, but I strongly suspected that he was wearing his usual ironic grin. Not wanting to appear foolish in his eyes, I plunged boldly forward through the water. A moment later, I experienced the most unpleasant sensation of my life: long river grass snaked around my legs, paralyzing my movements. I began to thrash around, panic-stricken.

"Watch out for the reeds—they're treacherous," Brett cried. "Keep away from them, for God's sake!"

But his warning came too late. I was already enmeshed in the grass tentacles. I was making a last desperate effort to free myself when something hard struck me. Dazed by the shock, I lost control of my movements and was carried away by the current. As I sank into unconsciousness, I felt myself going under, felt my lungs beginning to burst.

Chapter 10

I opened my eyes, and gradually my mind began to clear. After a moment or two, I recognized the slightly blurred face above my own as Brett's, anxiously bent over me. "How are you?" he asked, his voice slightly husky.

Still somewhat dazed, I murmured, "What happened? I had the feeling that someone was hitting me on the head to push me under." I brought my hand up to my temple, where I could feel a dull pain.

"You cracked you head against a rock as you were trying to free yourself from the reeds. You blacked out and were sucked under by an eddy."

"It's the first time that something like that has ever happened to me," I protested, and although I was burning inside with anger at myself, my voice sounded horribly weak. "That river is really treacherous."

My head was resting against his knee, and I suddenly noticed that his trousers were soaking wet. "You jumped in and pulled me out. You saved my life!" I blurted, overwhelmed with gratitude.

"Well, I could hardly stand there and watch you drown, could I?" he observed mildly. "You were all of about ten yards from the bank, I'd say, so at great risk to life and limb I jumped in and swam the few strokes needed to reach you."

I knew he was joking, probably to hide his embarrassment and to make light of what could have been a very nasty situation. "Nevertheless," I said quietly, "I really am very grateful."

"Think nothing of it," he replied gallantly. "Fished you out like a common trout, I did. But frankly, I think I'll stick to the real thing in the future. Trout give me more of a run for my money. You didn't put up any fight at all."

I still felt too weak to protest at this unflattering comparison. I had a sickly taste in my mouth. The muddy water I'd swallowed lay heavily on my stomach, and I felt a vague burning sensation in my throat.

"Can you walk?" he asked. "I don't want to hang around here any longer."

"Why not?"

He looked up at the sky. "It's after eight o'clock. We're in danger of running into people now."

Silently I cursed his unsociable character, his phobia of people. With some effort I got back on my feet. "I'll manage," I said. "I think I can go back on my own."

Ignoring my feeble protests, he bent down and swept me up into his arms. "Hang on," he advised, and I needed no encouragement. With my arms around his neck, I clung to him as he carried me across the river at a shallow spot only a short distance away. Being tall, I was no lightweight, but he carried me easily as though I were no heavier than a feather, and for the first time I realized just how powerful he was.

He lowered me to the ground on the other side, where I tottered slightly, still unsteady on my feet. "You're not going to black out on me again, are you?" he exclaimed, grabbing my arm.

I must have still been in a state of shock. "Give me a minute to recover," I pleaded.

I took a few deep breaths to steady myself. He looked at me intently with a mixture of anxiety and curiosity. His face, close to mine, glistened with drops of water. After a moment or two, I gave him a timid smile. "I feel better now," I said. "Thanks, Brett."

Picking up my dress, I hurriedly put it over my wet bathing suit, knowing that he wanted to be away from this open space as soon as possible. But then I started to shiver and vigorously he began to rub me down, scolding me like a loving brother. "You're going to catch the death of a cold," he admonished. "That was a very foolish and reckless thing to do, Dawn. Come on, now. Let's get going!"

He took me by the hand and together we walked up the path, back to his sanctuary. I was gradually warmed up by the sun and by the efffort of the climb. By the time we reached the Abbott's House, I was feeling a great deal better.

"It would probably be a good idea to take off your swimsuit," he advised. "It must still be damp." Tactfully he walked out onto the circular balcony while I proceeded to change my clothes. I'd brought some underwear in the picnic basket, and after I'd given myself another rubbing down with the towel, I got dressed again. My dress, I was pleased to note, had dried during the climb up.

"May I come back in?" Brett called from outside.

"Of course."

"Give me your swimsuit," he said, as he appeared in the doorway. "I'll spread it out with mine."

"Don't bother. It's already dry."

But he took it anyway, and hung it over the balustrade of the balcony.

"Well," he said, "after that little adventure, I think it's about time for us to have some breakfast. I see you brought something for the poor, starving artist," he added, nodding his head in the direction of the provisions I'd set out on the table. "Thanks."

"My pleasure," I assured him. "Let me give you a hand."

"Oh, no, you don't," he replied quickly. "You provided the food—the least I can do is provide the service." Then, in a more serious tone he added, "You've had a severe shock, you know. You should take it easy."

He picked up one of the wooden boxes he used for seats, carried it over to the Gothic window and set it down. Then he took a pillow from his bed and placed it carefully on the box. Meekly, I let him lead me over and sit me down.

Leaning against the warm, carved stone of the arch, I gazed out at the landscape drenched in sunlight. Then, closing my eyes for a moment, I gave a sigh of pure pleasure. "How good it is to be alive!" I whispered.

"As you now know, only too well," he remarked, his tone almost gentle.

"Was I really in serious danger?"

"Yes, you most certainly were," he replied emphatically. "You very nearly got sucked down into the Devil's Hole. It's a dangerous eddy, and many people have been lost in its depths. Once you get tangled in the reeds, you can't fight the current, and you get dragged under."

"So I could have drowned," I said with a shudder. "Thank God you were there, Brett."

He started to prepare breakfast things. As soon as the aroma of fresh-brewed coffee reached my nostrils, I felt fully recovered. He poured me out a large mug of it and added a generous amount of hot milk and sugar. A few minutes later he presented me with two golden croissants that he'd somehow warmed, along with a generous dollop of jam.

"You're very solicitous, all of a sudden," I remarked

lightly, both touched and surprised by his attention.
"Perhaps I should do that more often."

"Very funny," he observed dryly. "Next time I ll let
you drown. I ought to be angry with you for being so
reckless."

"Who would ever guess that there was a treacherous
Devil's Hole in such a peaceful-looking river?"

"You know, there's a saying: still waters run deep. But
why did you come down to the river in the first place?"
There was a mocking gleam in his eye that told me he
knew very well why. But he wanted to hear me say it.

I lowered my eyes, feeling suddenly shy. "You told me
you always went swimming in the early morning," I
murmured. "Today when I woke up, I suddenly felt like
going for a swim, too."

"A dangerous idea. But I thought you said you were
living in the lock keeper's house. If you'll forgive me for
pointing out the obvious, you've got what you need at
your back door. Why come all the way over here?"

"I hadn't seen you for three days," I said quietly. "That
seemed a long time to me."

"Touching," he murmured.

I raised my eyes to his, surprised that such a
potentially cutting remark should be made so gently. I
wondered what strange game we were playing. A blush
spread slowly over my cheeks; I felt confused and a bit
guilty.

Brett moved my makeshift chair out onto the balcony.
He went over and sat down on the crumbling
balustrade, letting his feet hang over the edge. His
tanned torso glistened in the sun. Under the bronzed
skin the muscles of his lean, hard body were clearly
defined. He looked very fit—and very attractive. I was
definitely attracted to him, that I couldn't deny, but not
just in the physical sense. The man was an enigma, and
he fascinated me.

As I tilted my face up to the sun, eyes closed, and let

the warm rays flood my face, I thought about how lucky I was to be spending the summer in the Périgord. It was golden.

"What are you thinking about?" Brett asked, interrupting my reverie. I realized then that we hadn't spoken for several minutes.

"I was thinking that it's good to have a friend," I replied.

"Because you believe in friendship?"

"Between a man and a woman? Why not? Aren't we friends already, the two of us?"

He didn't reply. He seemed to be preoccupied by something he didn't want to express. Turning his head, he looked at me closely, seemingly assessing me, as if trying to weigh the meaning of my words.

"You told me that you didn't know anyone here," he said finally. "And I find it hard to believe that you think of me as anything other than unexpected entertainment—the noble savage in his natural habitat." His words were bitter, his tone harsh.

Stung by this remark, particularly since it was not entirely wide of the mark, I struck back. "Why don't you just accept the fact that I like you?" I retorted sharply. "If I didn't enjoy myself with you, I wouldn't come here so often and intrude on your privacy." Which was entirely true, I thought, as I suddenly realized that it wasn't just curiosity about Brett that kept bringing me back here. It was Brett himself.

But I'd spoken in anger, protested too vehemently, and no doubt Brett had guessed the reason. But it was too late to retract it now. Already Brett had swung his legs over the balustrade and jumped down, and was now coming toward me. Hastily I lowered my eyes, waiting for the inevitable torrent of angry sarcasm to flood over me. And, I admitted ruefully to myself, it would be entirely justified.

But it never came, and as the silence lengthened in-

terminably I threw caution to the wind and raised my
eyes to his face. To my astonishment I found him gazing
down at me, a calm but thoughtful look on his face.
Then, almost imperceptibly, he shook his head. "No," he
murmured, as if to himself. "It would be too much to
ask a young thing like yourself to understand."

He turned abruptly, seemingly wanting to escape the
mood of the moment. I grasped him by the wrist.
"Please, Brett, what is it?" I pleaded. "What's the
matter?"

Roughly shaking himself free of my grasp, he turned
to face me again. "Matter?" he echoed, raising one
eyebrow questioningly. "Nothing—nothing at all."

"Oh, Brett," I protested. "It's obvious that you're worried
about something. Why else would you shut yourself away
from the world in this . . . this tumbledown old ruin?" I
gazed up at him, willing him to answer, searching his
face for some clue.

But it remained devoid of all expression. "I really
think," he said coldly, "that your near drowning this
morning must have affected your mind. Whatever gave
you the idea that I was worried about something?
Haven't you learned by now that I don't give a damn
about anyone or anything? And as for shutting myself
away in this 'tumbledown old ruin'—as you so elegantly
phrased it—I do it by choice, not from necessity. The
one thing in life in which I'm really interested in painting, and for that I need to be alone. You cannot give
your heart and soul to the job of covering an empty
canvas with a masterpiece if you're continually interrupted by unwanted guests arriving at inopportune
times."

He paused, then abruptly adopting a lighthearted
tone, he added, "And speaking of masterpieces, it's
about time we got back to your portrait. To work, my
beauty! You're here to pose: let's not forget it!"

His sudden shift of mood left me completely

bewildered and not a little upset. As he went back into the studio to prepare his materials, I had time to regain control of myself. But I'd been really puzzled by what I'd just seen and heard. I was now convinced, beyond a shadow of a doubt, that something *was* bothering Brett; that his choice of dwelling wasn't entirely due to an excessive desire for solitude. And I wanted more than ever to find out more about him.

Despite its inauspicious beginnings, this day was one of the finest we'd ever spent together. Brett proved to be excellent company—witty, talkative, almost merry. He seemed to want to allay my suspicions and make me forget the little incident that had had such an effect on me—on both of us. But I felt more strongly than ever that he'd allowed me a momentary glimpse into the depths of his soul, only to replace the barrier that separated him from me and everyone else.

I was happy in his company, yet still troubled by a vague uneasiness. I wondered if there was anything I could say or do to get him to confide in me. It wasn't any longer just idle curiosity on my part: I sensed that he was suffering, although it was difficult to guess from his outward appearance, and I wanted to help him. But he wasn't one to unburden his problems on others. He was jealous of his secret, even though I was sure it was festering within him.

The hours flowed by, each one filled with its own enchantment. I knew that I'd never be able to forget this day that had almost begun in tragedy. It would remain in my memory as a succession of perfect moments, like stepping stones exactly placed in some Zen garden.

Brett and I had lunch together in the corner of the tower, facing the sky and the enchanting rustic landscape. From our vantage point, we could look down over the forested valley to the terraced meadows, where cows and sheep grazed peacefully under the cloudless blue sky. We saw people going about their daily business—tiny dots, insignificant against the beauty and immensity of the landscape. In the distance we could see cars and trucks streaming along the main highway, and it seemed to me we were leaning over the balcony of heaven.

As I posed for my portrait, Brett amused me by telling me something about the famous people who'd come from the Périgord. Perhaps the best known of these was Montaigne, the great Renaissance author of moral essays. He'd been born in a château in this region. After an active life in Bordeaux he'd retired to his family estate to devote himself to literature. Montaigne's greatest friend, Etienne de la Boetie, was another native of the Périgord, who won fame as a poet and as a staunch defender of liberty. Brett also mentioned the great soldier and author, Pierre de Bourdeille, and was somewhat surprised to find that I knew of the man and had even visited his hometown of Brantôme.

But the historical figure that seemed to interest Brett the most was the beautiful Marie de Hautefort. A true femme fatale, she won the affections of the duke of Château Lherm and persuaded him to kill his innocent young bride of twenty-one, Marguerite de Calvimont. Inheriting his wife's fortune, the duke then married Marie de Hautefort, who lived in Château Lherm for the rest of her life, unpunished and unrepentant.

It was, in fact, a sordid tale of greed, adultery and murder. And as Brett spoke of this unpunished crime and of the wicked woman who'd inspired it, his voice became harsh and his face hardened in a strange, unexpected anger.

Though it was indeed an unpleasant story, I still couldn't really understand why he was getting getting so upset over it. To change the subject, I handed him his guitar and asked him to play for me. He sang a number of familiar folk songs and I joined in on the few I knew, my somewhat quavering soprano sounding absurd against his rich baritone. I recorded one of our duets on my tape recorder: I wanted at least one souvenir of this unforgettable day.

I watched the progress of the hours on the sundial at the top of the old tower and when, inevitably, the shadow touched the bottom of the sundial, I knew that it was time to go. I was still under the spell of this extraordinary day, and I had to make an effort of will to tear myself away.

Slowly and sadly I collected my things and got ready to go, putting off the unpleasant moment for as long as possible. Finally we said our goodbyes, and I made my way out of the abbey and down to my waiting car. For some reason I knew it would be a long time before I enjoyed another day so much.

Chapter 11

When I returned to the house, I found an invitation from Anne and Catherine asking me to join them for dinner that evening. They had a "proposition" they wanted to discuss with me.

I was delighted at the idea of spending the evening in such pleasant company, "proposition" or no, for I knew full well that I would only brood over my day with Brett if I spent the time alone. Hurriedly I washed my hair, changed into a clean, pale blue linen dress and set off in my car. I made it with a minute to spare.

Dinner passed pleasantly with a lot of general chitchat between Anne, Catherine, Bertrand—their brother—and myself. But no mention of the "proposition" was made, and by the time we adjourned to the living room for coffee, I was consumed with curiosity.

"All right, I give up," I declared, settling myself into an armchair. "I'm dying of curiosity. What is this proposition you have to put to me?"

Anne laughed. "It's nothing very exciting really," she replied. "It's just that we've agreed to help one of the local charities by lending them the château for a festival and historical pageant to raise money. We plan to take part in the show ourselves, and we wondered if you'd like to join us."

The idea appealed to me. As a foreigner, I was delighted to be invited to participate in a family project and to be treated as a friend rather than as a tourist.

"It's scheduled for this coming weekend," put in Catherine. "There'll be a festival run by our local priest. People will come to the fair from miles around, and they'll come to see the historical pageant. First we'll serve a buffet dinner on the lawn in front of the château. The show itself is a sound and light spectacular; it won't start until nightfall."

"It sounds wonderful," I said. "But how will you be able to feed everybody?"

"The young people are looking after everything," replied Anne. "Our job is to look after the pageant. We're going to make a grand entrance in a coach with four horses, dressed in period costumes to complete the illusion. We'd be delighted if you'd join us."

This prospect really did delight me. "I'd love to," I agreed enthusiastically, "but how on earth am I going to have a costume ready in time? After all, it's less than a week away."

Anne and Catherine gave me the address of a costume rental place in Périgueux where I could find something suitable to wear. Although suffering from a slight temperature, in spite of Brett's ministrations, I drove into town the next day, intending to make a quick stop at the costume-rental shop, then swing back to surprise Brett at the abbey and tell him all about the pageant.

However, during the drive to town, I changed my mind. I realized that I was spending far too much time thinking about him—much more than was sensible—and I had to control my impulse to seek out his company all the time. Besides, although Brett had expressed a desire to see me again soon, I wasn't at all sure he'd really meant it. Hadn't he mentioned something about "un welcome guests" at "inopportune times"? The last thing I wanted was for Brett to consider me a nuisance.

Well, I thought, *at least the pageant will give me something else to think about for a bit.*

And, indeed, my new project did help me to push Brett out of my mind. In Périgueux I picked out a magnificent embroidered dress in pale blue with a long train.

"It's fit for a princess," the saleslady exclaimed as I twirled in front of the mirror. I decided to take it. I also selected an elaborate period wig to go with it. With this costume, I thought, I'd be sure to make a fine contribution to the pageant.

When I had the complete costume in place, I once again examined myself in the three-sided mirror. I uttered a delighted cry of surprise at the elegant eighteenth-century lady who looked back at me. I thought what fun it would be to go to show myself to Brett like this. But then with a twinge of guilt I reminded myself that I'd promised not to think of him for a while.

I spent the next two days in feverish preparation for the show, running back and forth between the château and the lock keeper's house. Everything had to be worked out to the smallest detail so that nothing would be out of place. Bertrand directed the rehearsals for our grand entrance. A writer when the fancy took him—and when he could set aside time from his busy legal firm—he had personally prepared the script for the pageant. The château was full of bustle and excitement as an assortment of tradesmen and technicians hurried to and fro, making last-minute arrangements.

The parish priest, who'd originally thought up this idea for a charity event, was tearing around as if the devil himself were after him, directing the activities of the volunteer women and young girls of the parish, all of whom wanted to play a part in preparing for this grand occasion.

The château, hitherto so peaceful and calm in its setting by the banks of the Isle, was now filled with the uproarious presence of a crowd of young people who bubbled over with enthusiasm for their work. I found the change most pleasant and stimulating.

I was so caught up in the game that I didn't find any time to go to see Brett. When I thought of the unfinished portrait, a few guilt feelings would momentarily interrupt my general elation.

Anne and Catherine invited me to the château to spend the last evening before the show with them, to study the last details and receive our final instructions. We tried on our costumes. People were busy changing a ribbon, sewing on a piece of lace, pinning on a piece of paste jewelry or a flower.

As we worked we chatted. Catherine remarked with some sympathy that I had a "bit of a cough." Without thinking I said, "It's the result of a near drowning." And, since people asked me about it, I told them the story of what had happened, but without mentioning Brett's name.

"You really went swimming near the Devil's Hole?" asked Anne in astonishment.

I saw that everyone was looking at me in surprise. A bit embarrassed, I dodged the issue. "I'm a very good swimmer," I murmured.

"You have to know the area," Bertrand said. "It's very dangerous because of the reeds."

"I know," I replied. "I got caught in them."

"How on earth did you manage to escape?" asked Bertrand, lifting his eyebrows in astonishment.

"I was pulled out," I replied noncommittally, suddenly realizing that I was now treading on dangerous ground.

"Well, well!" one of the young women said jokingly.

"So you weren't playing water nymph all by yourself. You have a boyfriend that you're not telling us about."

Catherine shook her finger at me in mock admonition.

"Did he warm you up at last, after your enforced bath?" asked her sister.

Anne, I thought, *is really a bit of a tease.* I laughed Forgetting all caution I replied lightly, "We put on a burst of speed on our way back to the Abbot's House. It was uphill all the way, and by the time we reached the top, I was completely warmed up."

"You went to the Abbot's House?"

The drawing room was suddenly filled with an almost palpable silence that weighed on me like a stone. Looking around in alarm, I noticed the stunned faces of my hosts. They all wore the same expression of disbelief and near disapproval, as if I'd made a rude remark.

Catherine was the first to break the silence. Her classic features were strained and attentive as she said, "You're telling us he lives there?"

"Yes. What's so extraordinary about that?"

Everyone spoke at once.

"You must be mistaken; nobody lives in the Abbot's House."

"There's nothing there but crows—or ghosts."

"It's been abandoned for centuries."

On an impulse I was going to reply, "But Brett lives there, and he's not a ghost." But something held me back. I remembered how Brett had insisted I come alone, and how obstinately he refused to budge from his hideout. It came back to me that Emma had said much the same thing about the abbey. I decided it would be best not to mention Brett's name.

"Well," I said, as calmly as I could, "at the present time there's an inhabitant. The owner, no doubt."

"The owner's dead," Anne replied. "He let the abbey fall into a state of complete ruin. You can't even visit it without taking the chance of breaking your neck."

"But look," I protested, irritated by this stubborn refusal to believe me, "I've gone there a great many times to visit the man who lives there. I don't know whether he's the owner or the tenant, but the truth of the matter is that he lives there."

Just in time I stopped myself from adding, "He even does painting." I held my tongue, suddenly aware that for the past few minutes I'd been making a terrible fool of myself.

Bertrand looked up at me thoughtfully. "I think someone has been pulling your leg," he remarked slowly. "You should be more careful."

I wondered if it was really possible that these people didn't know anything at all about Brett—that they didn't have any idea that Brett even existed. But the Abbot's House, I realized, was very remote on its wild spur of rock. The thick forest formed a first line of defense and concealed the narrow pathway that gave access to the abbey. In any case, my friends at Château Donazac only lived there for part of the year, during vacations. They couldn't be expected to be aware of everything that was going on in the area.

I shrugged. There was no point in continuing this conversation at cross-purposes. I decided to say nothing more about my adventures at the Abbot's House—in fact I'd already said too much.

"Well, anyway, I'd better take it easy," I said with feigned nonchalance, for their remarks had upset me. "I'm still feeling a bit under the weather. If you don't mind, I think I'll retire. I want to be in top form for the long day tomorrow."

"You're sure you wouldn't like me to take a look at you?" The speaker was Dr. Dubois, an old friend of the family who'd been introduced to me during the course of the evening.

"No, thanks, doctor," I replied. "I'm sure a good night's sleep will do the trick."

With this exchange of remarks I took leave of my hosts. Anne saw me to the door. "You'd do well to go straight to bed, Dawn," she advised. "You're all flushed."

The conversation of the evening had worried me more than I cared to admit, and I really wasn't feeling completely myself. "Yes . . . I will. Good night, Anne. Thanks for all your kindness."

"Good night, Dawn. Just give us a call if you need anything. I'll see you tomorrow."

THE NEXT MORNING, I again realized how unpredictable the future can be. As I crawled out of bed after a night of fitful sleep, I found I was too weak to get dressed. I felt dizzy and nauseous, and as I took a few hesitant steps, I almost collapsed on the floor. I was barely able to reach the window.

Patrick was hanging around near the little boat. I tried to call him, but my voice was so weak and hoarse he didn't hear me. Finally, in desperation, I pushed one of the potted geraniums off the windowsill. The crash alerted him. I gave him a feeble wave, then tottered back to my bed. I was shivering uncontrollably and my throat seemed to be blocked by some kind of enormous lump, painful and suffocating.

Emma soon arrived. I begged her not to tell my friends at the château that I was sick; I didn't want to spoil their big day. People were already beginning to arrive at Donazac; young boys and girls were calling to one another excitedly, their voices carrying across the water, and from the direction of the highway, I could hear the tinkling of bicycle bells and the humming of car engines.

Preparations were in full swing for the big banquet on the lawn. A number of celebrities were expected—the Bishop of Périgueux, some important government officials, the local chief of police, an assortment of academics and a host of lesser luminaries.

"Don't tell them I can't be with them till the very last minute," I whispered to Emma. "Don't bother them before then. Do you think I could have some aspirin? My head is killing me."

Emma obeyed. I had only a minor role to play in the pageant: I was supposed to ride along in one of the carriages with a group of young ladies from the neighborhood. The carriage would get along fine without me, I decided. My absence would hardly be noticed.

I did feel sorry that I wouldn't have a chance to wear my blue princess's dress with its long train, or to see the sound and light show. But as soon as I'd taken a massive dose of aspirin, I forgot everything and sank into a deep sleep.

When I woke up it was already night. I could see a reddish glow through the openings in my shutters, and I heard the sound of loudspeakers. The château, I realized, must be lighted up by now, and the show must be starting. The joyous hubbub of the crowd drifted across the water, but I had neither the strength nor the desire to get up. I was consumed by fever and for some reason had the painful feeling of being lost, of being irretrievably separated from my mother, my family, my home—everything that I held dear.

I had been in France barely a month, but this was the first time I had ever spent so long a time so far away from home. Miserably, I thought of the eleven months I had still to go, and a sudden feeling of exile weighed heavily on my already troubled heart. In my fitful and feverish dreams all that came back to me were images of my childhood—our cottage in the country outside Montreal, the warm and peaceful room where I used to play with my brothers and sisters and, above all, the tender and loving ministrations of my mother when I'd been sick as a child. How I longed for her comfort now.

And still more of my dreams revolved around the Abbot's House. I was sickened by my own guilt. Had Brett not made it more clear he valued his privacy and seclusion above all else? And I had given the whole thing away—babbled on about the inhabitant of the ruined abbey—ignoring every opportunity to backtrack and cover my faux pas by saying I'd made a mistake. *Oh, Brett,* I thought in anguish, *have I ruined everything?*

Unconsciously, I moaned. "Do you want something to drink?" someone asked immediately.

Emma leaned toward me, a worried look on her face. Behind her, a bearded man was looking at me. I closed my eyes, too weary to reply. There was something around my throat that made me feel as if I was being strangled. I later learned that Emma had been unable to get the drugs prescribed by the local doctor, because the druggist in Neuvic had closed shop to attend the festival. Resorting to an old folk remedy, she'd wrapped some warm ashes in a nylon and wound it around my neck. From time to time, she replenished the nylon with ashes taken from the kitchen stove, which she'd taken the trouble to light.

The bearded old doctor went away, shaking his head. Emma remained at my side. Out of the goodness of her heart, she'd decided to miss the dazzling spectacle of the illuminated château, the pleasures of the banquet and the festivities that were being consummated in an atmosphere of laughter, rejoicing and delight.

Dear Emma, I thought. I realized now that beneath their crusty exterior, the people of the Périgod had hearts of gold. I wasn't about to forget her generosity and devotion.

I soon sank back into a feverish state. My mind wandered, and at times I wasn't even aware of where I was.

I remained in this condition for almost an entire week. Anne and Catherine came to see me every day, bringing me clear broth, medicines and, as soon as I felt better, magazines asnd newspapers. They showed me photographs of the festival: it had been quite a production and I was sorry I'd missed it.

Gradually I recovered from what had been a very severe throat infection. After nearly a week in bed, I was back on my feet and taking my first hesitant steps in the garden.

The next day, Anne called for me and took me for a long drive in the country. It was a beautiful day and she put down the top on her Alfa Romeo. She handled the small sports car with surprising skill. As we drove along beside the still waters of the Isle, she pointed out a number of old châteaus and told me stories, legendary or historical, that were associated with each one.

I was particularly delighted when we stopped to visit the château of Jumilhac, once the home of the renowned warrior Du Guesclin, who'd driven the English out of the Périgord many centuries ago. In the château we saw the so-called "Room of the Spinner," where legend had it that a beautiful woman had been locked up by her jealous husband. She'd spent forty years of her life there, in solitary confinement, spinning wool to pass the time. Finally, she pined away and died, leaving her self-portrait on the wall of her prison. *Men*, I thought to myself.

For the next week or so either Anne or Catherine drove me everywhere and I enjoyed their company tremendously. Both young women were full of life and their continual banter and laughter soon overcame my fit of depression. And I was particularly delighted to be shown around the area by two people who knew it so well, for they showed me many of the local delights I would never have found for myself.

The first thing I did one beautifully sunny morning

when I was once again strong enough to take the wheel of my own car was to drive over to see Brett. I imagined that he must be wondering why I hadn't visited him in so long. Perhaps he thought I wasn't coming back at all. I was looking forward to giving him a pleasant surprise—at least, I hoped it would be a pleasant one. I was still mortified by my indiscretions of a couple of weeks ago.

I drove through the forest in the direction of the Abbot's House, passing Delacour Manor on my right. I realized with a jolt that, for some time, I'd forgotten all about the Sleeping Beauty castle. I remembered what my brother had asked me to do and I promised myself to stop in on the way back and find out if Alys had returned yet, and if not, when she was likely to do so.

Soon I came to the faded road sign and turned off onto the bumpy road that would take me through the densest part of the forest to my friend's abode.

I came to a bend in the road where it narrowed and became little more than a track. As I came out of the curve, I had to slam on the brakes suddenly to avoid hitting a car blocking the way—a black Mercedes. Some adventurous tourists, I suspected.

That will please Brett, I thought, smiling to myself as I imagined him hiding himself away in the labyrinthine ruins of the Abbot's House to avoid the unwelcome intrusion. If these people thought they were going to catch Mr. Bear in his hideout, they were sure to be disappointed.

I pulled my little Renault over to the shoulder and parked it under the trees to leave the road clear. Climbing out of the car, I headed off in the direction of the abbey on foot.

I'd only walked a short distance when I heard a murmur of voices. There was a crunch of footsteps on the gravel, and a moment later I found myself face-to-face with two people coming from the opposite direction.

I stood rooted to the spot, overcome with astonishment. "Alys!" I cried.

She stopped dead in her tracks. We stared at one another for a second, each of us shocked to find the other there. "Miss Charbonneau! Dawn!" she exclaimed finally. The surprise in her voice masked, I sensed, less innocuous feelings. "You're still here?"

"Didn't I tell you that I'd rented a house?" I said lightly, managing to recover my composure more rapidly, I thought, than she. Boldly I returned her stare. In the depths of her startling green eyes I detected a ripple of agitation.

She gave me a quick, forced smile. "Oh, yes, you did tell me," she admitted. "I'd forgotten." She frowned slightly, half closing her eyes.

"Did you have a nice trip?" I asked her in bland politeness.

"Yes, thank you. I only just got back. By the way, what are you doing in this remote place?" she asked, abruptly changing the subject. I was beginning to think it was her favorite pastime.

She spoke softly, but her voice contained a hint of subdued hostility. But I didn't have the time to take offense, for her companion suddenly stepped forward. In a resonant, authoritarian voice he said, "Aren't you going to introduce us, my dear?"

I turned to look at him. He was an immense hulk of a man, with a booming voice and an imperious manner. He was carrying a package under his arm and his white sports jacket was cast negligently over one shoulder. His open-necked shirt revealed the matted hair on his powerful chest. His face was swarthy and had a pair of the nastiest-looking eyes I had ever seen, narrow and heavy lidded. I took an instant dislike to him.

"Dawn, this is Mr. Charles Courtney. Charles, this is

Dawn Charbonneau," Alys said ceremoniously. "Charles was a friend of Maurice," she added, rather defiantly I thought, as though afraid I might not approve.

I looked at them warily, wondering at the relationship between them. I was so confused that for the moment I didn't think of asking them what they were doing there.

Alys was the first to break the awkward silence. "Miss Charbonneau was also a friend of Maurice," she told her companion.

"The sister of a friend," I corrected her. "My brother and Maurice were very close. They were friends from their college days."

Obviously Alys considered this a delicate subject she had no wish to pursue, for once again she quickly changed the subject. "Are you taking a walk around the area, Dawn?" she inquired. It was the same question she'd asked me earlier, but at least this time it was more politely put.

I had no choice but to answer her. Not wanting to reveal the true purpose of my visit, I replied noncommitally, "Yes, I'm just having a look around. It's a very picturesque spot, isn't it?"

"I don't know if I'd call it picturesque," she replied cooly, looking around her with an expression of evident distaste. "It's wild and practically inaccessible. You're likely to get lost if you don't know where you're going."

"Oh, I doubt that," I contradicted airily. "I thought it might be fun to do some exploring around here. I noticed the road sign on the first day I came to your place."

"You have good eyes," she remarked coldly, narrowing her own to stare at me thoughtfully. "That sign is so faded it's barely noticeable."

The conversation began to take on the air of a cross-examination. Her catlike green eyes searched my face, and I realized I couldn't let down my guard for a minute. "I'm very fond of this area. I hope to explore every part of it," I said evasively.

We must have made quite a picture, planted in the middle of the road as if neither of us could make up her mind to let the other go past.

The resonant voice of Charles Courtney suddenly broke the train of these reflections. "You came by car, I presume?"

I turned toward him. "Yes, I left it a little way down the road from yours. That's your black Mercedes, isn't it? I didn't have enough room to get past," I said pointedly.

"You wouldn't have been able to drive much farther, anyway," retorted Alys quickly. "The road is very bad."

"One thing about my little Renault—it can go just about anywhere," I reassured smugly, just to annoy her.

"I don't suppose it can climb up rocks?" she queried caustically, a self-satisfied look on her coldly beautiful face.

"Well, maybe not," I admitted. "But I don't mind exploring the rest of the way on foot.

Her eyes lingered on me speculatively. I presumed she was wondering if I was coming here for the first time, or if I knew the area better than I was letting on.

"Wouldn't you like to come and have coffee with us at the manor?" she offered, suddenly turning on the charm. "It'll give us a chance to renew our acquaintanceship."

It was a chance I could well have passed up if it hadn't been for Norman's request. "Why, thank you very much," I replied, feigning surprised delight. "Now that I know you're back, I'll drop in and see you. I have a request from my brother that I want to pass on to you."

"Well, then, why wait?" she continued smoothly. "Let's all go back to the manor now." Casually she took hold of my arm, as if to make me turn around.

Oh, no, you don't, I thought grimly, gently removing it from her grasp. I wondered why she was so keen to get me away from the area. "Please excuse me," I said, "but I'd rather not come over just now. I love going for walks and and I'd like to look around a bit more while it's still so nice out."

Her face darkened in anger. "But don't you know," she said severely, "that you're on a private road?"

"It's the first I've heard of it. Is it part of your estate?"

"Well, no," she admitted, chewing her lower lip in annoyance.

"In that case," I remarked cheerfully, "don't worry yourself on my account. If I meet up with the owner I'll just turn on the charm. I'm sure he won't eat me." And I favored her with one of my most dazzling smiles.

Alys's mouth became a taut line and she took a deep breath, as though about to reply. But Charles Courtney's large hand moved forward almost imperceptibly and touched her elbow, cautioning her not to be too insistent. She seemed to heed his warning. Changing her expression and her tone, she said pleasantly, "All right, then. I hope you have a nice walk, even though there's nothing up there but a heap of old ruins. But we'll have a glass of wine waiting for you when you've finished your wanderings. You promise?"

"Thank you. I'll be there." I had to accept the invitation: it seemed the only way to get rid of them.

The prospect didn't exactly thrill me, but I had promised Norman I'd find out as much as I could about Maurice's death, and this afternoon seemed as good as time as any to question Alys further on this subject.

I thought of Brett, suddenly eager to see him again. Perhaps he could tell me something about Alys and her unpleasant companion. There seemed to be some connection, after all, between my hermit in his eagle's nest and the inhabitants of Delacour Manor.

Brett had never said anything about Delacour,

although I'd occasionally mentioned it in conversation. But Alys's presence on this road seemed to indicate that she went to the Abbot's House from time to time to visit her neighbor.

And now that I thought of it, the bulky package under Charles's arm looked suspiciously like rolled-up canvases. I wondered if there was some kind of relationship between Charles and Brett. I didn't think Courtney was quite Brett's type, but it seemed reasonable to suppose that Brett had decided to sell some of his paintings and had, perhaps, hired the man as an agent.

Momentarily reassured by these reflections, I walked on more rapidly, eager to make up for lost time. Alys and Charles disappeared around the bend in the road, and a few minutes later I heard the faint but unmistakable sound of a car engine moving away through the forest.

I hastened on, growing more impatient by the minute. The only sound to break the silence of the deserted landscape was the crunching of my footsteps on the flint rubble of the path. Then the Abbot's House came into view and I felt suddenly apprehensive. It looked so desolate and lonely.

When I reached the stone staricase leading to the chapel, I cried out, "Brett! Hello, Brett, where are you?"

There was no reply. The crows, alerted by my approach, lumbered off into the air, cawing in annoyance. I wondered if Brett was spying on me from his usual observation post by the Gothic arch, hidden by the dense ivy. Perhaps he was purposely avoiding me, angered at my long absence. Or it was possible, I thought, that he was off painting somewhere in the ruins and hadn't heard me.

I climbed the stairs. From time to time I called out, "Hey, Brett! Are you deaf or sleeping?"

I hurried through the uninhabited rooms of the abbey, then climbed the narrow, concealed staircase leading to the attic studio. I'd hoped, at least, to run into Sarah, but she was nowhere to be found. When I finally reached the top of the stairs and stepped into the studio, I knew immediately that something was wrong. It felt abandoned, devoid of human presence.

Gingerly I took a few steps forward, full of uneasiness. There had been a number of changes since I'd last visited the place. The bed was folded up, leaning against the wall, useless, as though ready to be carted away. The blankets, pillows and sheets had disappeared, and there wasn't a trace of the kitchen utensils that Sarah had used to prepare Brett's simple meals. The little stove was pushed over into a corner, like a piece of scrap iron. Brett's painting equipment and his canvases had all vanished.

Of Brett himself there was no sign at all. It looked as though some unknown person had come here and ruthlessly removed every trace of his presence.

I was crushed, almost grief stricken by the inescapable truth: he wasn't there anymore. Brett had completely disappeared.

Chapter 12

I was overwhelmed. I'd been ready for anything but this—an attack of bad humor, reproaches for my long absence. But this unexpected situation left me completely stunned and demoralized.

I wondered what could have happened to bring about his totally unforeseen departure. More than ever, it was forcefully brought home to me that I really knew nothing about Brett. I didn't even know his last name. And now there was nobody to ask. Sarah, the only person who could tell me something about him, was a complete stranger. I didn't have the faintest idea where she lived, or how I could get in touch with her. Brett had vanished into thin air, leaving not a single clue behind to guide my search for him.

The Abbot's House had reverted to what it must have been before he came—the ruined abode of ghosts and crows.

I was more shocked than I'd have thought possible. I realized that I'd just lost someone who was dear to me, a friend who, in the few weeks I'd known him, had won a place in my life and in my heart.

The silence was abruptly broken by a sound. It was a

moment before I realized it was my own voice, whispering, "No, it's not possible! I don't believe it!"

But it was not only possible, it was an incontrovertible fact. I felt indignant, bitter and somehow betrayed. The fact that I was all alone and far from home, I realized, was one of the reasons that I was taking all this so personally. As I reflected on the unexpected turn of events, I had to admit to myself that Brett's departure might have a perfectly reasonable explanation. After all, he was a grown man, a free agent; he could come and go as he pleased. But I still couldn't understand why he hadn't thought of notifying me of his decision. Had I been nothing more than an insignificant passerby in his life?

It was that thought that hurt the most, the thought that my visits and our happy hours together might have meant so little to him that he could leave without even saying goodbye. I tried to shake myself out of my mood of despondency. *Come on*, I chided myself, *don't be such a sentimental fool. You're getting all worked up over the disappearance of somebody you didn't even know a couple of months ago.* I'd told Brett I'd rented the lock keeper's house for the summer. He could have got in touch with me if he'd wanted to, and if he hadn't, he obviously didn't attach any importance to our friendship.

In spite of my efforts, I didn't seem to be able to get a grip on myself. I couldn't tear myself away from this studio to which I'd grown so attached, even though the spirit of the place had fled. With my elbows propped up on the balustrade of the balcony, I cast a last melancholy glance over the magnificent landscape that had, on so many occasions, offered me the promise of friendship and warmth. I could almost feel Brett beside me still. His mysterious presence, which had at first intrigued me and then won me over, was very much alive in my memory.

I suddenly realized just how much I was going to miss him.

I felt like leaving the Périgord. All at once it had lost its charm for me. I wiped an angry tear away from my cheek, silently rebuking myself for my folly. I had to stop feeling sorry for myself because I'd lost Brett, so I summoned all my courage to shake off my depression, to banish him from my thoughts forever.

Ashamed of my weakness, I threaded my way back through the ruins, willing myself to indifference. My heart wasn't in it, but I managed to hum a little tune to myself. I was sorely tempted to turn around and bid a last, fond farewell to the ivy-covered Gothic arch from where Brett had so often watched for me. But I found the strength to resist.

However, as I went past the chapel my obsession returned, triumphant. I remembered my first meeting with Brett and I couldn't hold back my feelings any longer. I felt frustrated, unhappy, close to tears. My lips trembled. I stumbled along beside the crumbling walls, gazing unseeingly at the dense thorn bushes that seemed to guard the approach to the place.

I noticed, amid the gray green leaves, a light spot of color. I stared at it for a moment, blankly, trying unconsciously to figure out what it was. And then, as if guided by a sixth sense, I went over to it, my curiosity aroused. As I picked it up, I finally realized what it was: a roll of canvas, tied with a piece of cord, that I recognized immediately. The last time I'd seen it, it had been hanging around Brett's neck, holding a silver pendant that he often wore.

I untied the cord and unrolled the canvas. It was my portrait.

My heart started to pound. I examined the painting, holding it away from me and then bringing it up close. Brett hadn't wasted any time since our last meeting: he'd finished the portrait from memory. It was, I saw, a very good likeness in a highly original style, and once again I was struck by the talent that Brett undoubtedly possessed.

At the bottom of the painting, Brett had lettered in the title: Portrait of the Friend.

This chance find had an overpowering effect on me. Coming so soon after my attack of doubt and resentment, it released a flood of joy that was as inexplicable as my earlier depression. Rapidly I recovered both my serenity and my confidence. So Brett had thought of me! He had remembered my face during my long absence and had captured it on the canvas, tenderly and with great attention to detail. The knowledge touched me deeply.

Dear Brett, I thought. I did mean something to him, after all. I was the Friend, with a capital letter. There was a special place for me in his secret heart.

Which, when I thought about it, made it all the more difficult ot understand why he had left without a word to me about his departure. And why, I wondered, was this canvas here? Why hadn't he taken it away with the others? I raised my eyes toward the abbey. The bush where I'd made my discovery was placed just under the window where so often Brett and I had dreamed together. I realized that if someone had thrown the carefully tied canvas out that window, it would have fallen at the very place where I'd picked it up.

But who, I wondered, would have thrown my portrait out the window, so that it would be concealed in the bush? Who, if not Brett himself? But why? That was the truly puzzling question.

Sitting down on a nearby stone, I began to reflect on the situation. I remembered Charles Courtney and the package he'd been carrying when I'd met him on the road to the abbey—the package I'd thought looked like rolled-up canvases. Let's suppose, I thought, that Brett hadn't removed the paintings, that someone else had taken them, instead. Perhaps, for some reason I couldn't even begin to guess at, Brett had found himself in a situation where he couldn't take them with him.

There were, I thought, two possibilities then. Either he'd hidden my portrait to keep it from the prying eyes of people he didn't trust. Or—and at this point I considered it the more likely possibility—he'd had to leave in a hurry and had found this way of telling me he hadn't forgotten me.

Dawn, the romantic, I thought with a grin. But I was convinced I was on the right track. My grief-stricken stupor had vanished and my mind was fully alert. I felt a heady excitement that urged me to act.

My discovery of the canvas had thrown a whole new light on the situation. This image of me, which Brett's talent had created, was some kind of message, some sort of clue that would eventually lead me to him.

In a flash I realized what I had to do. The one person who I was sure knew something about Brett's disappearance and could explain it to me, was his neighbor, Alys. When I'd met her on the road, she'd obviously been coming back from the Abbot's House that she'd been so eager to keep me from reaching.

There was no doubt in my mind that Alys had known that Brett was living in the abbey, and that the attic of the tower was his hideout. Now all I had to do was to find out why he'd left in such a hurry, and what part she'd played in his sudden disappearance.

"A GLASS of white wine would be lovely," I said.

Alys brought me my drink. She was all sweetness and charm, and I didn't trust her a bit. She seemed all too eager to convince me that whatever had been worrying her when we'd met near the abbey was long since forgotten.

I sipped my wine. As she was pouring herself a

surprisingly stiff Scotch, I took another look around the drawing room of Delacour. My gaze fell on the now familiar grand piano, the pieces of period furniture and the massive Louis XIV armchairs with their velvet upholstery.

Directly across from me, on the wall above the fireplace, I saw the portrait of Roland Laurensac, the cousin from Mexico. He seemed to be staring out at me in open curiosity.

"I'm going to tell Charles you're here," Alys announced, starting to get up from her chair. "I'm sure he'd like to come and join us."

I grabbed her firmly by the wrist. "I'd like to speak to you alone for a minute, first," I said.

She removed her arm from my grasp and stared at me. It seemed to me—though this was perhaps nothing but a fancy of my suspicious mind—that she paled somewhat.

"Ah, yes," she said, quickly recovering her composure. "You mentioned that there was something your brother wanted me to do for him."

"I'm not talking about that right now," I replied. "I'd like to ask you a question: what happened to Brett, the artist who was living in the attic of the Abbot's House?"

This time she shuddered visibly. She ran her tongue nervously over her lips, but her voice was firm and steady when she replied, "I don't know what you're talking about. The Abbot's House is a ruin. It's been uninhabited for centuries."

"There was a man living there only a couple of weeks ago," I contradicted quietly, "on a permanent basis. He even had one of the local women to come in to do his housework. I want to know what happened to him."

I had to admit she was a consummate actress. Perhaps her nostrils did become a little pinched at my words, but otherwise she showed very little sign that my words had affected her in any way. "What absolute nonsense!" she declared scornfully. "Who on earth fed you that pack of lies?"

Now I started to become angry. "It's not nonsense," I retorted sharply, "and I didn't get the information from anyone. For over two weeks I went to see Brett almost every day. Then I got sick and couldn't visit him. And when I went back today, he was gone. It's no use your trying to deny it, either," I continued coldly, raising my hand imperiously to stem her protestations. "You know very well what I'm talking about. When I met you out there in the woods this morning, you couldn't possibly have been coming from anywhere except the Abbot's House, and you seemed remarkably keen to keep me away from it."

Now she did react. In fact, she almost staggered under the impact of my words, as though she'd been struck in the face. Her lovely features contorted and her face darkened in sudden fury, her green eyes glittering fiercely. She raised her hand, and for a moment, I thought she was going to strike me. Alarmed, I half raised my arm to ward off the blow. But then she managed to regain control of herself: her hand, with its slender fingers and long red nails, moved to stroke the side of her neck.

"You've been very, very foolish," she said slowly, her voice low. Her eyes were hard, icy.

"Foolish? Why?"

"Brett didn't tell you?"

"He didn't tell me anything very much," I confessed, rather reluctantly. "All I know is his first name and the fact that he likes to paint. In fact, he painted my portrait."

She stared at me for a moment in disbelief. Finally she let out a long sigh, as though resigning herself to the situation. Her face, which had looked almost ugly when distorted by anger, now relaxed, and her features resumed their cold beauty. Grasping her glass, she hastily downed its contents, then stared at it silently for a few minutes, turning it around in her hands. Finally, very deliberately, she placed it on the table and looked up at me.

"Miss Charbonneau," she began heavily, "I'm afraid I'm going to have to tell you something that you're not going to like. You've got yourself involved in a very unpleasant situation you'd be far happier not knowing anything about."

"I know Brett's a bit unsociable and secretive, but I don't think he was particularly bothered by my visits. Quite the contrary, in fact. I rather got the impression he enjoyed my company once in a while. It seemed to amuse him and to do him some good."

She laughed bitterly. "Do him some good, indeed!" she exclaimed, maliciously imitating my Canadian accent. "You're a fool, Dawn! Nothing can do him good now, especially not you, a stranger who knows nothing about him. You don't know what risks you've run."

Risks? What on earth was she talking about, I wondered. Never, for one moment, had I felt any danger in Brett's company. Nevertheless, as I stared at Alys in astonishment, seeing her face once more contorted with emotion, a cold chill ran down my spine. Surely this could not be entirely acting on her part.

"What are you trying to . . . tell me?" I stammered, not really wanting to know, but impelled to ask all the same.

"Just this," she replied, and I could have sworn I detected a note of triumph in her voice. "Brett is insane—stark raving mad. He's already killed one person, and who knows what he might have done to you had I not put a stop to his little game. He was living at the Abbot's House, because he'd escaped from the mental hospital. In fact, you were here the night they came

looking for him, remember? I told you that they'd come
to tell me someone had escaped from the hospital that
afternoon, but it wasn't just someone. It was Brett."

My mind filled with horror as I recalled the events of
my first night in the Périgord. In my mind's eye, I could
see the living room as it had looked then, dark and
shadowy, with thin beams of moonlight gleaming in
through the windows. I could feel again the pounding of
my heart as I'd heard the window blow open. Or had it?
Perhaps someone had tried to get in after all—Brett,
trying to break into his own house in the middle of the
night. And I remembered my puzzlement at the car, the
silent group of shadows, the sudden flight and pursuit.
But I wasn't puzzled now. As the pieces of the jigsaw
were slowly put together, the whole ugly picture was
laid out before me with startling clarity.

"No, no!" I whispered. "I can't believe it!"

"It's the truth," she said harshly. "Everybody knows
how Maurice died: Brett killed him. And it may help
you to realize the enormity of the crime when I tell you
that Brett's last name is Briançon. Yes—" as I gave a
sudden cry of disbelief "—Maurice was Brett's brother,
and Brett killed him. Now do you understand?"

I sat there petrified, unable to move or speak, stunned
by this horrible revelation.

As in a dream, I saw Alys lean toward me. I made a
halfhearted, childish gesture of dismissal, then abruptly
burst into tears.

For once, Alys acted as the perfect hostess. She got up
and went out of the drawing room, leaving me to
struggle with the emotions that were engulfing me. I was
thankful that I wouldn't have a witness to my breakdown for, despite my anguish, I was highly embarrassed
at losing control of myself in this manner.

Many minutes went by before I was able to come to
terms with the shock. Alys's words still resounded in my

ears: "Brett killed Maurice. . . . Brett is insane." It was too much to take in. How could I possibly accept something so monstrous?

I remembered Brett and his strange way of life. I'd always known he was carrying the burden of some secret in his heart. Now I knew what that secret was. No wonder he'd avoided people like the plague and had seemed so horrified at the prospect of human contact.

In my company he hadn't behaved at all like a madman, although I'd always known there was a streak of violence beneath the usually superbly controlled exterior. I had always found him to be rational and highly intelligent. But then, I knew that people who are completely insane can, at times, act in a perfectly normal manner. And I hadn't been with him all that much. Perhaps his madness only manifested itself in periodic outbreaks. . . . I just didn't know what to think.

Gradually I began to recover some measure of self-control. Alys had not returned and I was still alone in the drawing room. I got up, went over to a mirror and dabbed at my swollen eyes. In the reflection I noticed the figure of Charles Courtney appear in the doorway. I glared at him balefully, with mixed hostility and mistrust.

"Excuse me," I said, a great deal more calmly than I felt. "I'm just on my way out."

"I don't want to impose on you, Miss Charbonneau," he said smoothly, "but as a legal adviser and friend of the family; I have a few things to say to you and I hope you'll be willing to hear me out. Mrs. Briançon has asked me to explain these matters in which you have so unfortunately become involved."

I thrust my compact back into my purse, walked back to the chair on which I'd been sitting and picked up my coat. "I don't want to know anything more," I replied firmly. "I'm just very sorry that I got mixed up in 'these matters,' as you put it. If only I'd known!"

"But how could you know?" he said, affecting a placating smile. "It's not your fault at all, we quite understand that. Through a series of unfortunate events, you've become aware of a family tragedy. For everyone's sake, I would advise you not to say anything more about it."

"If you think for one moment I'm going to gossip about this, you're sadly mistaken!" I snapped, furious at his implication. "That's not my style, believe me. I just want to forget, if I can."

He drew closer. "Now, now, my dear," he said hastily. "Of course I didn't mean to imply that you'd be indiscreet in any way. However, now that you know part of the story, I think it would be best if you heard the rest. If only so that you can tell your brother."

"I'd rather not tell my brother anything about it," I retorted. But I had to admit that it wouldn't be easy to keep the truth from Norman.

Gently but firmly Charles took my coat and bag and placed them on a chair. Then, taking me by the arm, he steered me over to the sofa and made me sit down. By now I was too emotionally exhausted to protest; in any case, his manner brooked no opposition.

He sat down on the other end of the sofa, and adopting what was no doubt his best barrister's manner, said, "My dear, you've had a severe shock and I wish I could help you. However, I feel it's my duty to give you a full report on the tragic events that have befallen this family. I realize it's distressing, but it's quite necessary. And I'm sure that later on during the course of your vacation, you'll have plenty of opportunity to make up for these few unpleasant moments."

Much he knew, I thought. Considering the state I was in, I was quite sure I'd never forget this day as long as I lived, much less "make up" for it. However, I tried to keep my composure. After all, I had to face reality, no matter how terrible it was.

Charles unfolded his story in long, resonant phrases, gesturing with his hands and putting in plenty of rhetorical flourishes. He must, I thought, be highly effective in court. But what he had to say to me was so horrible, so tragic, that his pompous manner seemed entirely out of place.

"Maurice returned to Delacour after his grandmother died," Charles began. "He intended to settle down on the family estate, but within a very short time came into conflict with Brett. Brett's always been a little odd, you know: he never cared much for people and hardly ever left the estate after his return from military service. He was hit particularly hard by his grandmother's death and became more and more withdrawn. When Maurice arrive with his young bride, Brett immediately took a dislike to her, which only aggravated the tension between the two brothers. They were so completely different in every way.

"That situation soon changed," Charles went on. "Brett suddenly fell violently in love with Alys. He never said so openly, of course, but he used to follow her around everywhere like a puppy. He was completely devoted to her and couldn't stand to hear anyone criticizing her in any way. The fact that Alys and Maurice had a falling out made matters even worse.

"I'm sure you can understand the antagonism between husband and wife," Charles continued. "Alys is young; she's lively, gay, fond of social life. But Maurice had had enough of that kind of life in Paris, and he wanted to live permanently at Delacour. Alys wasn't pleased with his decision. They had words. During the course of one of their arguments, Maurice acted a bit violently toward Alys and Brett intervened. He jumped on Maurice and pushed him into the corner of a wall. Maurice struck his head very hard and died a few days later from the injuries he'd received."

"And Brett wasn't arrested?" I asked in surprise.

"Well, I'd like to think that my modest talents had something to do with that," he replied pompously, looking away from me slightly in a very pretty, but entirely affected, gesture of humility. "Besides, Maurice didn't want to press charges against his brother. What he did do, however, was discuss the incident with the hospital psychiatrist, who agreed to give Brett a complete psychiatric examination. Happily for all concerned, Brett submitted to the examination, the outcome of which was that he was deemed not responsible for his actions. He was committed by the psychiatrist to a local private hospital for mental patients, but as you know, escaped from there a few weeks ago. They looked for him, but nobody thought of searching the Abbot's House, where he'd taken refuge in the tower. An old country-woman, Sarah, who you've probably met, was party to his concealment. She'd been employed at Delacour for many years and had always had a soft spot for Brett.

"Frankly, they didn't look too hard for him while Alys was away. They wanted to check with her before bringing attention to the escape with their search. The director of the hospital is a good friend of the family, and he was trying to keep the whole thing quiet. He didn't want to drag this tragic affair into the public eye again. Brett is not violent unless he's upset, so his 'being at large,' as it were, didn't put the local people in any kind of danger. Remember, too, that Brett hasn't been formally committed, and Alys is solely responsible for his acts. When she returned she took the matter in hand. She had a pretty good idea of where he was hiding and went to see him herself. She didn't have any trouble persuading him to go back to the hospital."

"She persuaded him?" I queried, now completely astonished. I couldn't believe my ears.

"Certainly," he replied firmly. "Brett returned of his own free will. He knows very well that he can't remain at liberty, at least, not until he's cured. His insanity is intermittent, and when he's lucid he feels the full burden of horror and remorse for what he's done."

Poor Brett, I thought. *He has so little to look forward to.* I wondered if he fully grasped the magnitude of the tragedy that had overwhelmed him.

I stood up with some difficulty, feeling unsteady on my feet. I managed to say, "Thank you for telling me all this. I'll be going now. Please forgive me if I've bothered you, and convey my apologies to Mrs. Briançon."

"You mustn't hurry off," Alys said gently. She was standing in the doorway. "I've had a place set for you. Stay and have lunch with us. That will give you time to recover from the shock."

"No, thank you," I replied firmly. "I'm going home to pack my bags. I'll leave for Paris tomorrow. I don't want to stay here one day longer."

My declaration was greeted by silence. Alys and Charles looked at one another, and perhaps it was my imagination, but I could sense a feeling of relief between them. Perhaps they had found the retelling of this tragic story as difficult to relate as I had to hear. Certainly, they didn't insist that I stay and join them for lunch.

My head was beginning to clear, and all at once I felt ashamed of my recent behavior. "It's high time I returned to Canada," I said stiffly. "I don't want to prolong my stay in France."

"I understand," Alys murmured. "I think that's a good idea."

"I do, too," added Charles.

They accompanied to my car. "Do you want me to give you a lift to the train tomorrow?" he asked, almost eagerly.

"Thank you, but you needn't bother. I have to return the car to the rental agency, anyway."

As I took my place behind the wheel, I noticed that my knees were still trembling. But I managed to assume an outward air of calm dignity. They stood there watching me as I hastily drove off. In my rearview mirror, I saw them go back into the house, the tall, heavily built man and the slender woman.

At the end of the driveway, I stopped the car and lighted a cigarette with trembling fingers. I'd suffered a terrible shock to the nervous system and was still shaking. I didn't feel strong enough to drive all the way back to Neuvic immediately, and decided to make a detour through the forest.

I drove off again. When I passed by the place where the dirt road branched off to the Abbot's House, I made a great effort to keep my eyes firmly fastened to the road ahead. But I couldn't keep myself from casting a glance in the direction I'd taken so many times, my heart carefree and gay.

The road sign bearing the faded name of the abbey, I noticed, had been removed. But the ache in my heart continued unabated. Brett, the one man I loved—yes, I would admit it now—more than anyone else in the world, was a madman and a murderer!

Chapter 13

My first inclination, as I'd told Alys and Charles, was to leave, to get away from the Périgord and its now unhappy memories as fast as possible. Accordingly, when I arrived home I spared only a distracted glance for the lunch Emma had prepared for me before going straight up to my room to start packing.

I felt terribly confused. Aimlessly I wandered around the room, unable either to realize what was happening to me or to decide what to do.

Thus, when Emma showed up after lunch to wash the dishes, as she did every day, she found me in the midst of a great disorder of suitcases pulled out of closets, drawers left open and clothes tossed every which way. "What's going on here?" she cried, throwing up her hands in astonishment.

"I'm leaving, Emma."

She stared at me wide-eyed. "You're leaving? Where to? Why, you haven't even had lunch!"

"I'm not hungry," I said flatly.

"Don't be silly. I've made you some nice braised veal in sorrel sauce and it won't keep. It's no good when it's reheated."

"You can take it away, Emma. I won't be eating it. I'm leaving for good."

"For good? You mean you won't be coming back at all?" She stared at me, her mouth wide open in astonishment.

I nodded.

"But you've rented the house until the end of August, and it's only the beginning July!"

I shrugged. "I'll just have to lose a month's rent, that's all. That's not too serious."

"What's happened?" Emma whispered. She was obviously at a loss to understand this strange decision of mine.

"I think I'm going back to Canada," I told her.

"You've received bad news?" she asked, alarmed.

"No, Emma, but I miss my family. I . . . I guess I'm not the world traveler I thought I was. I find I'm quite lonely and little bit depressed."

"You? Depressed? But you're always so cheerful! It's your cold. You're still not completely over it. Wait awhile, it'll pass."

Emma wanted so much to persuade me. She tried a smile, hoping to cheer me up. Stubbornly I stuffed a pair of shoes into a bag, unmoved by that good woman's attempts to change my mind.

She took a few hesitant steps among the suitcases scattered on the rug, as if to go. Then she came back toward me, inspired by a new idea. "What about the ladies at the château?" she asked. "Aren't you going to see them, the ladies? They'll persuade you to stay, I know they will."

"I'll go to see them," I replied, "but only to bid them farewell."

Farewell. It was such a dismal word. Emma started to cry. "Oh, Miss Dawn," she pleaded, "don't talk like that. One would think some misfortune had happened to you. You look so sad."

A misfortune had happened to me, I thought. I'd just lost a tenderness that was beginning to fill my heart. I cast a tearful glance in Emma's direction. She was wiping her eyes with the corner of her apron and dabbing at her face.

Dear Emma, I thought. *She thinks I'm leaving on a whim and she's hurt.* I felt badly that I'd made her feel so sad and disappointed.

I put my arm around her. "Emma, I'll never forget your kindness," I told her.

"Why are you leaving, then? Did somebody do something to you?" At this new thought, her face took on a grim, almost fierce, expression. She looked ready to do battle with my enemies, whoever they might be.

"No," I replied. "Everybody has been very kind to me."

She stopped in front of my portrait, which I'd unrolled and placed on top of the chest of drawers. Frowning in concentration, she studied it for a moment, then turned to scrutinize me. "My," she said, "but that looks like you. One would say . . . would say it's really you."

"Yes, Emma, it's me," I sighed.

"What a fine likeness! One would think you were going to speak."

"Do you know where this portrait was done, and by whom?" I asked suddenly.

She looked at me in puzzlement. "How would I know?" she said.

"It was done in the Abbot's House by the man who was living there—Brett, the brother of Maurice Brian-çon, of Delacour Manor."

Emma's face suddenly took on a wary look. "Dela-cour," she muttered darkly. "You've been to see that woman again!"

Obviously Emma didn't trust Alys any more than I did.

Trust! Abruptly I sat down on the bed, struck by a sudden awful thought. What was I thinking of? What I'd been told by Alys and Charles might, conceivably, be true, but why should I accept without question the words of two people whom I barely knew and didn't trust? I'd only heard their side of the story. The least I could do for Brett was to give him the benefit of the doubt until I'd heard his side, too.

But just how was I going to accomplish that? It would be relatively easy to find out where the mental hospital was, but I wasn't at all sure I'd be allowed to see one of its patients. After all, I wasn't even a relative.

Sarah! I had to find Sarah. Perhaps she, at least, could tell me something.

I jumped to my feet, excited at the idea of positive action for a change. "Emma," I said quickly, "do you know a woman in the area called Sarah?"

"Sarah," she repeated, wrinkling her brow in thought. "I remember there used to be a Sarah at Delacour, but—"

"That's the one!" I interrupted excitedly. "Do you know where she lives now?"

"No, Miss Dawn. That's the odd thing. She left Delacour some months ago and nobody's seen or heard from her since. She was always a secretive soul and we never paid much attention to her. Liked to keep herself to herself, she did."

Finding Sarah was obviously not going to be as easy as I'd hoped. "Listen, Emma," I said decisively, "I've changed my mind. I'm not going to leave—at least, not right now. But I've got to find Sarah. I know she's in the neighborhood somewhere, and you know the people around here better than I do. What's more, they'll trust you more than they will me. If you could do me a big favor and make some discreet inquiries around the area for me, I promise I'll put all this stuff away and there'll be no more talk of leaving. Is it a deal?"

Obviously delighted by the fact that I would be

staying on a little longer, Emma readily agreed and bustled off downstairs.

She came back up a remarkably short time later with a mysterious look on her face. "There's someone downstairs to see you, Miss Dawn," she announced. "She's waiting in the kitchen."

"She?" I queried. Emma couldn't possibly have found Sarah so quickly. "Who is it? A lady?" I suddenly thought of Alys and gave an involuntary shudder.

"No, not a lady. A woman."

In Emma's vocabulary, "lady" was an elegant woman who dressed in the latest fashion. A "woman" on the other hand, was one of the local country folk who wore the traditional dark headscarf and apron.

"What does she want?" I asked.

"To speak with you."

"Tell her to come up."

I was intrigued. I heard some discussion below, and then, to my complete astonishment and delight, Sarah suddenly appeared at the door to the bedroom. I hadn't had much time to clear up and it was still in a complete state of chaos. Taken aback by the mess, she looked around her suspiciously. "You're leaving?" she asked.

"I was thinking of it," I conceded.

"Oh!" Her body stiffened in a gesture of silent disapproval.

I rushed over to her. "Thank God you've come!" I exclaimed. "I didn't know where to find you. I'm so glad to see you"

We stared at one another in silence, sharing the same thought. Two tears ran down Sarah's cheeks. "So," she said simply, "you're leaving him."

Her face was pitiable to behold. I smiled down at her. "No, Sarah," I said gently, "I'm not leaving—not yet, anyway."

"If you leave there'll be no one to help him."

"You know, I may not be able to do anything for him, anyway," I warned her.

"But he's not responsible!" the old woman exclaimed.

"Exactly. If what I've been told is true, then he's not responsible for his actions. That's why he's been deprived of his liberty. I think we both have to face facts, Sarah, however u..pleasant they may be. He may not be normal."

"Bah! Not normal!" she spat contemptuously. "Do you really believe that? Why, you came to see him almost every day. Did he ever seem 'not normal' to you? I should know. I'm the one who raised him."

From what I had seen of Brett, I had to admit I was inclined to agree with her. But perhaps both of us, each devoted to Brett in her own way, were being blinded to the truth by our love for him. And if I hadn't seen Brett escape from his guardians with my own eyes only a month or so ago, I would have dismissed Alys's and Charles's story as the most outrageous piece of fabrication I'd ever heard. As it was, a modicum of doubt remained in the back of my mind.

Sarah buried her face in her hands. "My poor boy," she sobbed. "Nobody wants to help him."

"But I *do* want to help him, Sarah," I said gently. "That's why I'm staying after all."

She looked up at me, hope dawning in her mind.

"What happened, Sarah?" I asked. "How did they find him?"

Her eyes flashed angrily. "It was her," she said. "She's the one who found him. Only she knew that he'd once set up a studio in the attic of the abbey. As soon as she came back from her trip and they told her they hadn't been able to find him, she knew exactly where to look."

"But I still don't understand how they persuaded him to go back to the hospital. Alys's friend, Charles Courtney, told me he went back of his own free will."

"Free will, indeed!" she scorned. "She set some kind of trap for him, you mark my words."

"Were you there when Alys came for him?"

Sarah was sobbing again. "No, I came to the abbey one morning . . . there was nobody there. She'd taken everything away—his pictures, his brushes, your portrait."

"No," I said, pointing to the canvas of the chest of drawers. "My portrait's here."

She stared at the canvas and stopped crying. "How did you get hold of it?" she asked.

I told her the story. She nodded her head vigorously. "That's just like my Brett. He'd have thrown it out the window so it would land in the bushes and she wouldn't see it. He was very fond of you."

Her face reflected a new resolve. "You're not going to let this go on, are you?"

"What?"

"Keeping Brett a prisoner in that hospital."

"I'll do what I can," I promised, not knowing what else to say. "But I'm going to need your help. All I know so far is what I've been told by Alys and Charles Courtney. I've got to hear Brett's side of the story. Have you any idea what happened that night between him and his brother? I'm sure that's the key to the whole thing."

Sarah shook her head. "It's a pity that *madame* isn't still alive," she said angrily, pressing her handkerchief against her swollen eyelids. "She'd soon put things to rights. But maybe it's just as well she didn't live to see this."

I became curious about Brett's past, of which I knew nothing. I moved a chair over to the window. Very slowly, with all the tact I could muster, I maneuvered her over to it and got her to sit down. "How could all this have happened?" I asked. "Did Brett, in his childhood, show any signs of . . . well, any kind of mental illness?"

"Never in his life!" she cried. "I spent twenty-two years in service at Delacour, and my parents were there before me when the grandmother was alive. I was a child, then. After I got married, I continued to work there regularly when extra help was needed. Then, one harvest season, my husband was kicked by a horse and died. Brett had just been born, and old Madame Delacour asked me to come to the manor to raise the little one."

"What about his mother?"

"Young Mrs. Briançon lived far away, with her husband. He had something to do with the diplomatic service. They traveled a lot. We hardly saw them, except for the summer. Most of the time only Mrs. Briançon came. She returned home to have the baby, but she went away again and left it with us. We didn't see her again for some time.

"When her husband died, she came back. Brett was three or four. She didn't leave again. She shut herself up in Delacour like a nun. She didn't want to see anybody. She was always sad, and she stayed in mourning for her husband right up to the day she died. Brett was twelve then. The grandmother continued to look after him. She didn't want to become separated from him, even to send him away to school. He went to the village school, and afterward a teacher came to give him private lessons. His grandmother arranged a special tutor to give him art lessons when he'd displayed an interest in it. Brett showed the signs of great talent early on, and he used to spend hours on his own, painting and painting." Sarah paused, as if picturing those long-ago days. "He only left Delacour to do his military service. . . . He had a funny sort of life."

I listened avidly to what she was saying. The information provided by Sarah threw a new light on the situation. I tried to imagine what it must have been like for Brett, growing up in the depths of this solitary manor, with only his widowed mother and grandmother for company. Surely that might have been enough to drive any man a little crazy.

I wondered where Maurice fitted into the picture. When I asked Sarah, she said, "Mr. Maurice left the house when Brett was still a child. There was ten years' difference between Brett and himself. The two brothers never had much to do with one another. Even before Maurice left for college, the boys were seldom together. Maurice had always gone with his parents on their travels. Later on, he was in boarding school in Paris. When he finished school, he went on to university, also in Paris, and he rarely came home to visit. When he got married and started his business, he came even less.

"His wife didn't like it here, and old Mrs. Delacour didn't care for her. When the old lady died, they came down more frequently. Maurice decided he liked it here and wanted to move back to Delacour. By that time, I hardly went to the manor anymore. I'm getting old, and I left my service some months ago. My sister, who's also a widow, operates a little farm, and I help her. I only came to work at the abbey because Brett needed me."

I was fascinated by the strange ways of this family. I didn't remember Maurice ever talking about his family to Norman. Of course, I might not have known if he had: I'd been very young when Maurice had visited us.

Sarah got up. She gave me a searching look. "Well," she said, "are you going to look after Brett or not?"

"I'd like to," I replied slowly. "But I really don't know where to begin. After all, his family had him committed."

"His family! You mean that she-devil of a sister-in-law of his? It's awful the way she manipulates him. What's her hold on him, anyway, that's what I'd like to know?"

"According to Charles, he's in . . . love with her," I remarked bitterly. Was he still, I wondered.

"In love with her!" echoed Sarah, obviously completely taken aback. "Why, that lying, pompous . . . ." Here, she hesitated, seething with indignation, and groping for the right words to describe her low opinion of Charles. Failing to find any to her satisfaction, she continued, "He never trusted her from the moment he first laid eyes on her!"

"Never trusted her?" I queried, astonished, and not a little delighted by this revelation. And now that I came to think about it, the idea of Brett following Alys around like a love-starved puppy seemed ludicrous in the extreme. In fact, I would have laughed out loud at the idea if the situation hadn't been so serious. Brett was certainly not the type to advertise his feelings in such an extraverted manner.

I was struck by a sudden thought. "But how—" I began.

"Exactly," interrupted Sarah darkly. "How does she do it?"

"And why?" I added.

"That's easy," replied the old woman unhesitatingly. "Money. Brett inherited the estate when his brother died. If she can get Brett out of the way, she can do what she likes with the property. She'll have control."

This explanation didn't entirely satisfy me. Why would Alys be so anxious to take possession of a property she hated? Then it occurred to me that if she sold it she might get quite a bit for it; according to Brett, places in the Périgord were much sought after by fashionable Parisians. But surely Maurice left her some money. . . . I asked Sarah.

"Who knows?" She shrugged. "If he did, perhaps it wasn't enough. . . ."

"Doesn't Brett have any other family?" I asked.

She thought for a moment. "Well," she said finally, "there was old Mr. Laurensac, his mother's distant cousin from the Mexican side of the family. He sometimes came with his son Roland, who was about the same age as Mrs. Briançon. They used to spend their summers in the Périgord, and were very fond of young

Brett. Brought him some wonderful presents, they did. They were very well-to-do. But when Brett's mother died they stopped coming and nobody's heard of them for years. I did hear tell that the old man had died, but I don't know what happened to Roland. He'd be about sixty now, I guess."

She shook her head sadly. "No, there's nobody left to defend Brett, and to keep him out of the clutches of that tigress."

Tigress, I thought, was a singularly apt description of Alys, although with her cold dark beauty and hard green eyes, perhaps panther would have been more appropriate.

"But we're forgetting one thing," I remarked, more to myself than to Sarah. "Brett is supposed to have killed his brother. Surely even Alys wouldn't lie about a thing like that."

She raised her arm, and her wrinkled face flashed with anger. "It's not true!" she insisted. "Maybe they did fight, I don't know, I wasn't there. But Maurice died of an injury he did to himself, when he fell and struck his head against the wall."

"Nevertheless, if Brett did, indeed, start the fight, and he is mentally unstable—"

"That's nonsense!" Sarah said defiantly. "There's nothing unstable about Brett." Then suddenly her face crumpled, and she began to cry. "I only know that my little boy is shut up in a horrible place, an insane asylum, and he's not any crazier than you or I. But nobody cares enough about him or to do anything about it. Nobody!"

Oh, yes, I do, I thought grimly. I suddenly realized I had to see Brett again. My conversation with Sarah had raised enough doubts in my mind to convince me that there was more to this whole, ugly situation than I'd been told so far. And I was determined to get to the bottom of the mystery, if it was the last thing I did.

Chapter 14

At first I thought of going to ask Alys to give me permission to visit Brett. I was sure that I'd never be allowed into the hospital without her consent, since she was responsible for his committal. But when I mentioned my idea to Sarah, she was dead set against it. Alys, she argued, would never agree to help me, and she'd do everything she could to keep me from seeing him. And when I remembered the relief I'd sensed in both Alys and Charles when I'd told them I would be leaving for Paris, I was inclined to agree with her. It would be best to keep them in the dark.

Thus, we had to concoct some plausible reason for me to see Brett without Alys's permission. Sarah left me in charge of this, saying that she had to get back to help her sister. We made plans to go to the hospital together the next day—she would show me the way—and when we'd completed our arrangements, she left.

As soon as she'd gone, I was once again filled with misgivings. I wondered what kind of situation I was getting myself mixed up in. I was, after all, a perfect stranger, and wondered if I had any right to involve myself in such a delicate family matter. I didn't have any legitimate reason for introducing myself to the doctor who was looking after Brett. I was just a chance acquaintance that Brett had happened to fancy as a model.

I studied my portrait, trying to think of some plausible excuse for visiting the hospital, something that would convince Brett's watchdogs. Suddenly, it came to me: Brett had forgotten to sign his name on the canvas. I could say that I wanted to see him so he could sign his name on the painting.

The next morning, Sarah and I climbed into the little Renault and headed off in the direction of the clinic. It was only a short distance away. A few minutes later, I turned onto the property and drove up a beautiful driveway lined with ancient walnut trees. As I pulled up in front of the hospital, I realized that there was nothing in the external appearance of this Renaissance château to suggest its real function.

A discreet plaque informed me that it was indeed a private clinic for mental patients, and that the director was one Dr. Kloster.

I had to talk to a number of nurses and secretaries before I reached the doctor, but all of them were extremely polite and friendly. Finally I was ushered into a large office with a high carved ceiling and a magnificent antique fireplace.

The doctor was an elegant, immaculately dressed man of middle age. He studied me with interest while I described myself as a Canadian journalist who'd been assigned to the Périgord to look for material for TV programming. He seemed convinced by the story: his face relaxed and his manner became less guarded.

He fetched me a high-backed chair and brought me an ashtray. Sitting down behind his desk, he said, "Well, what can I do for you, Miss Charbonneau?"

Boldly I went to the heart of the matter. "I'm here to see one of your patients, Brett Briançon. His brother, Maurice, who I understand passed away recently, was a dear friend of my brother's. Brett honored me by painting my portrait while he was still at liberty."

Dr. Kloster's face tightened at the mention of Maurice. He frowned slightly and examined me closely as I spoke.

Affecting the most casual air, I continued, "I went to see Mrs. Briançon, who told me that I could find Brett here. I was going over my things in preparation for my return to Paris when I noticed my portrait wasn't signed. I'd very much like Brett to sign it for me, so I just popped over here."

I unrolled the painting, which I'd been carrying under my arm, and showed it to the doctor.

"As far as I can tell, this man has a great deal of talent," the doctor remarked, evidently impressed. He spread the portrait out on the desk and examined it carefully.

I wasn't there to discuss Brett's artistic merits, but I humored Dr. Kloster for a moment, waiting to see what would happen next. I was still worried that I wouldn't be allowed to see Brett and I was boiling with impatience.

"A moment ago you said something that I would like to comment on," the doctor murmured enigmatically.

Here we go, I thought. I braced myself for a lecture to the effect that the condition of the patients made it impossible to allow visitors under any circumstances.

"You said," he continued, "that Brett Briançon did your portrait 'while he was still at liberty.' But he is always at liberty."

"What do you mean? He's not here?" I asked in consternation.

"Oh, he's here all right. But this hospital isn't a prison. All our patients are here of their own free will. They haven't been forced to come here. They're more or less aware of their condition, and they know that we can help them to get better. Brett is in this situation."

"But he escaped—about, oh, two months ago," I

protested, stunned by his remarks. "And some attendants were sent to Delacour to catch him and bring him back. You call that free will?"

Dr. Kloster looked both hurt and surprised by my accusation. "I assure you, Miss Charbonneau," he said severely, "that no one from here was sent to 'catch him and bring him back,' as you put it. In fact, we didn't even send anyone over to Delacour to advise Mrs. Briançon that he'd left the hospital. There was no need. Mr. Courtney arrived here that afternoon with his assistant, and—"

"Courtney?" I echoed, interrupting him rather rudely. "Charles Courtney?"

"That's right," confirmed the doctor. "He's the family lawyer and has been a great help to both Brett and Mrs. Briançon throughout this whole tragic affair. Anyway, he arrived at the hospital with some papers for Brett to sign. As a matter of fact, that's how we found out that Brett had gone. Normally, when our patients leave, they advise us ahead of time, but Brett disappeared without saying a word to anyone. Mr. Courtney very kindly offered to convey the information, via his assistant, to Mrs. Briançon for us, and we left it at that. I knew Mrs. Briançon was going away for a month or two on the following day, so I didn't expect any results until after her return. And that, in fact, was the case. She returned Brett to us the day after she arrived back."

As Dr. Kloster talked, I became more and more bewildered. "And you didn't send two orderlies out that same night to bring him back?" I inquired when he finished.

"Certainly not," he declared emphatically. "That would be completely against our policy. And as I told you, Mrs. Briançon didn't bring Brett back for two months. That is not an extraordinary occurrence with our patients, Miss Charbonneau. They often sign themselves out for months at a time. But whatever gave you that idea?"

I didn't answer. I needed time to absorb and think over what I'd just heard before committing myself any further.

Deciding it was time to get back to the business at hand, I pushed the doctor's startling revelations firmly to the back of my mind. "Do you think it would be possible for me to see Brett for a few minutes?" I asked.

"Certainly," Dr. Kloster replied without hesitation. "He's staying in one of the smaller buildings on the grounds. I can't let you go there, because outpatients don't receive visitors in their own quarters, but we have a visiting room in the main building here. You can wait for him there. I'll have him brought over."

I felt astonished, even a bit confused. I hadn't thought it would be as simple as this. "Thank you," I said, unable to repress a sigh of relief. "I'll take you up on your kind offer."

"I have only one recommendation," he added. "Don't say anything to excite him. We advise against it: it could bring on an attack."

"Is he really mentally ill, doctor?" The question slipped out unbidden.

He shrugged. "It is not appropriate for me to discuss my patients, Miss Charbonneau. Let's just say he appears excitable and prone to violence. For the moment, he's under observation, and I can't give you a definite answer at this time. He seems to suffer from obsessional problems, which in his case seem to be partly justified."

He didn't offer any further explanations. Showing me out of his office, he led me to a large sitting room where armchairs and sofas were set all around the walls. "Brett will be brought to you," he said. "Please wait here a moment."

My temples throbbed and my hands felt sticky. I was

going to see Brett again, and in what a place! However, I had to admit that the atmosphere of the clinic was very unhospitallike; it was even a bit reassuring. I walked over and glanced inquisitively through one of the high windows. I noticed some newly constructed buildings on the grounds, surrounded by flower beds. There was nothing forbidding or depressing about the place, and it was hardly what I'd expected. If it weren't for the nurses walking along the pathway in their white uniforms, it could be taken for a resort hotel, inhabited by perfectly normal people.

I sat down in one of the armchairs. I'd picked up a magazine and was abstractedly leafing through it, in a vain attempt to calm my nervousness, when I heard the door open. There was a rustle of skirts, and I heard a voice say, "Here's your visitor."

"Dawn!" came a sudden, startled exclamation. Obviously I was the last person Brett had expected to see.

I looked up as the nurse who'd accompanied him to the visiting room smiled and went out, closing the door gently behind her. It seemed to me, as I gazed at him fondly—lovingly—that Brett had never looked more handsome. The faded, paint-stained blue jeans and rumpled shirt had been discarded in favor of a pair of well-cut gray flannel trousers and a crisp white silk shirt that contrasted vividly with his raven-black hair and his deeply tanned skin.

I got up and gave him a shy smile, but he failed to respond to my overture of friendship. "Why have you come?" he asked sharply.

"To . . . to see you, of course," I stammered, somewhat taken aback at his cool reception. "I thought you might like a visitor."

"You thought I might like a visitor?" he echoed, his voice filled with scorn. "In this godforsaken place? You must be joking!"

"Brett, please!" I implored, suddenly on the verge of

tears. "Don't spoil it for me. It's so good to see you again."

"Well, now you've seen me—the monkey in its cage," he said harshly. "So, if you'll excuse me, I've got things to do."

For a moment, I simply stared at him in disbelief as he turned and walked toward the door. Then, abruptly, I burst into tears. Brett's cruel words had cut through me like a sword, and I could no longer stem the flood.

All at once I felt the light touch of his hands on my shoulders. I buried my head against his broad chest. "Dawn, Dawn," he murmured softly, gently stroking my hair. "I didn't mean you to take it so hard."

"Oh, Brett!" I moaned between sobs. "How can you say that when you know I . . . love you."

I felt him stiffen suddenly, and cupping my chin in his hand, he raised my head. For a few eternal seconds, he gazed down at me intently, his somber gray eyes sweeping searchingly across my face. Then his arms dropped limply to his sides and he turned away, a look almost of horror on his face. "Oh, my God," he whispered. "What have I done?"

Completely bewildered, I gazed at his broad back, feeling a great coldness within me. Could he really be mentally ill? *No*, I said to myself, *it's not possible*. I remembered all the weeks when I'd seen him almost every day. He was a bit eccentric, perhaps, different from other people. But surely, I thought, some of his peculiarities could be explained by his artistic nature.

"What are you talking about, Brett?" I asked. "You haven't done anything—at least, not to me."

"Do you know I killed a man?" he asked in a hollow voice, his back still toward me. "My own brother!"

"I heard something to that effect," I admitted. Remembering the doctor's warning, I kept my voice as calm as possible. "But, as I understand it, it was an accident, albeit an unfortunate one."

He swung around to face me, and I had to admit I was taken aback at the sudden fury showing on his dark face. His gray eyes flashed with anger. "As you understand it!" he sneered. "An accident caused by my own uncontrollable violence! And you say you understand it?"

But even in this outburst, I couldn't see him as abnormal. What man, I wondered, wouldn't be affected by such a tragedy?

"Do you really feel sick?" I asked, gazing at him intensely, defying him to say yes.

"The doctors seem to think I am."

"*Seem* to think?" I repeated, becoming angry. "You call that a diagnosis? What do the psychiatrists say?"

"Oh . . . ." He gave a slight, somewhat contemptuous shrug. "They ask me questions. They study me. They attempt to probe my mind for answers. So far, they don't seem to have had much success in finding what makes me tick."

"Well, there certainly wasn't anything the matter with you when I visited you at the Abbot's House," I remarked.

"Obviously you don't know much about mental illness," he returned swiftly. "Even the most insane people in the world can act normally at times."

This uncomfortable truth had occurred to me, but I pushed it firmly to the back of my mind. "But I saw you practically every day for a period of several weeks," I objected. "You always seemed relatively normal to me."

"Relatively!" he echoed, pouncing on the word. "You see, even you had doubts at times."

Mentally I kicked myself for being so stupid. "No, that's not true, Brett," I protested vehemently. "Never once did I feel in any danger when I was with you."

"Kind of you to say so," he remarked sarcastically. "All that proves is that I can be normal and lucid—"

"As you are being right now," I pointed out, interrupting him as a sudden, sneaking suspicion crept into my mind. Could he be feigning his illness? If so, why?

"Remarkably so, I might add. Oh, come, Brett," I continued, still angry. "I'd have noticed something sooner or later. I admit at first I thought you were a little obsessive about your privacy, but that was explained when I learned that you'd escaped from this place. Understandably you didn't want to be seen. Other than that, you didn't seem the least bit sick. I heard you laugh, freely and openly. Sarah told me you slept very soundly. That's not the behavior of a mentally disturbed person. And I don't see why you have to bear the full responsibility for the death of your brother. You fought and he was the one who fell, but it could just as easily have been you. It was a kind of duel between you— from what I heard. I don't want to excuse what you did, but surely Maurice was as responsible as you were for what happened."

I was saying anything that came into my head, in a desperate effort to persuade him to level with me. I was becoming increasingly sure that Brett was not only completely normal, but also was innocent of Maurice's death. The only thing I didn't know was why he was trying so hard to convince me, and everyone else, of the exact opposite.

I had no idea why I felt this way. Perhaps Sarah had transmitted some of her blind faith to me. But equally, I realized that much of the reason probably lay in the fact that I loved Brett so much I just couldn't imagine him guilty of such a crime.

"As far as I'm concerned," he said quietly, "Sarah has a mother's blindness, and you—" he looked down at me almost tenderly "—all the indulgence of a friend. I appreciate your concern, Dawn, believe me, but I'm afraid there isn't much you can do about heredity."

"Heredity!" I echoed in surprise. "What on earth has heredity got to do with it?"

He gave me a wry smile and began to pace up and own the room. "It's a nasty little secret the Briançon family has managed to keep mainly to itself over the years," he replied. "I hate to disillusion you, Dawn, but my father was incurably mad. In fact, he died in an insane asylum.

"So you see," he continued softly, stopping in front of me, "I really am Mr. Bear—a bear that has to be kept in its cage. I may seem gentle enough at times but, like a bear, I can suddenly turn vicious."

Abruptly he turned and walked over to the window. An oppressive silence filled the room as I painfully digested this new and unpleasant revelation. Could it be true, I wondered, or was this merely another effort on Brett's part to convince me he was mad?

From somewhere outside the grounds, I heard a sound I hadn't noticed before: one of the patients was singing a plaintive song, a song without words, haunting and melancholy.

"That damned song again!" exclaimed Brett irritably. Suddenly he turned to face me. "You shouldn't have come here," he said fiercely, "into this atmosphere of paranoids and mental deficients. Why did you come?"

"To try to help you," I replied evenly. "To try to figure out a situation I don't understand. Your excuse that your father died in an insane asylum just doesn't wash, Brett. Not all mental illnesses are hereditary. Certainly no one ever suggested that Maurice was insane. Why should you be any different? I refuse to believe that you could have changed so much in so short a time. Just a few weeks ago, we were spending whole days together. We got to know each other well and became friends. And you never revealed any abnormal tendencies."

"You just never realized it," came the short reply.

"Rubbish!" I retorted. "You're no more insane than I am, and the idea of your losing your temper involuntarily is laughable. A more self-controlled man would be hard to find."

"Stubborn little thing, aren't you?" he remarked caustically.

"Yes," I agreed firmly. "And I'm not going to be sidetracked, either. Brett, what are you doing in this place? Why have you let yourself be brought here?"

"Haven't you heard?" he drawled. "This is a mental hospital, which, in case you didn't know, is where they put mad people like me. I did come here of my own free will, you know."

"That's another thing I don't understand," I put in swiftly. "What hold do Alys and Charles have over you that they managed to persuade you to come back here, to a place you obviously loathe and where you don't belong?"

For a moment I thought I had him. For one short instant, surprise registered on his face. Then, just as swiftly, it was gone, to be replaced by a faintly wary look. His eyes narrowed slightly as he asked, "Just how well do you know those two?"

"Enough to know I wouldn't trust them farther than I could throw them," I retorted.

"You surprise me, Dawn," he drawled, his noncommittal tone just a little too perfect. "Hasn't anyone told you how devoted my dear sister-in-law is to my well-being? Why should you feel so differently about her than anyone else?"

"For one thing, I don't like people who lie," I replied calmly. "And for another, I happen to know that it was Charles, or someone in his employ, who came to warn Alys that afternoon in May that you . . . escaped from here. Having been assured by Dr. Kloster that he didn't send anyone out after you that night, I can only assume it was Alys and/or Charles who arranged that little reception for you."

Now I did have the satisfaction of seeing his face

register surprise. "Might I inquire how it is that you're
so conversant with the events of that fateful night?" he
asked acidly.

"I just happened to be in the drawing room when you
tried to climb in the window," I replied matter-of-factly.
"Only I didn't know it was you until yesterday. The
next morning when I questioned Alys about it, she just
told me someone had escaped from here. She didn't say
who."

"So it was you who scared me half to death that
night," he murmured, shaking his head as though he
found it hard to believe. "I thought it was Alys lying in
wait for me, especially when I heard the car coming up
the driveway."

"I wasn't exactly a model of calm myself, you know,"
I reproached him. "Brett, what were you and Maurice
fighting about the night your brother was injured?"

For, if I'd learned nothing else during the course of
our conversation, Brett's comments about Alys and
Charles had at least told me one thing. He no more
loved his sister-in-law than I did. In which case, Charles
had lied; Brett would not have attacked Maurice merely
because Maurice had quarreled with his wife.

He refused to answer my question. "You already
know so much about the incident," he replied coldly.
"I'd be surprised if no one bothered to mention that."

"Maybe they did," I conceded, refusing to be drawn,
"but I don't always believe what I'm told."

But he still refused to answer, so I shifted my attack.
"By the way," I said casually, "why did you return to
the house that night? Were you looking for something?"

Again he refused to answer. Instead, he strode swiftly
over to where I was standing. "You'd best forget all
about me, Dawn," he said softly. "Through my stupidity
and selfishness, I've got you involved in a situation you
know nothing about. I'm truly grateful for the friendship
you've shown me, but you're better off without me,

believe me. It may be months, even years, before I can get out of this place, and—"

"But you don't belong here," I cried. "Why should you stay here any longer?"

Suddenly, without warning, his arms shot out and he grasped me firmly by the shoulders, his long fingers biting into the tender flesh. "Fool!" he said fiercely. "Why do you insist on putting so much stock into a relationship that can bring you nothing but misery? For the last time, I am mad, Dawn. Do you understand? I—am—mad!"

Dropping his hands from my shoulders, he turned, strode swiftly over to the door and opened it. "Goodbye, Dawn," he said softly. "Thank you for everything."

And then he was gone.

Chapter 15

I spent most of the rest of the day lying on my back on my bed, hands behind my head, staring unseeingly up at the ceiling.

I'd left the visiting room of Dr. Kloster's private clinic feeling completely wrung out by my encounter with Brett. For one thing, I'd had the strong conviction that, in his own mind at least, his "goodbye" had been final, and that certainly hadn't made me exactly cheerful. Then, too, there had been his stubborn refusal to answer some of my more probing questions. In fact, I had learned absolutely nothing from him that made any sense at all.

He had, at least, confirmed that he neither liked nor trusted Alys any more than I did, which, I suppose, gave me some small measure of comfort. But it also made it all the harder to understand why he bended to her will so readily. Perhaps he was, after all, just a little bit mad. Could he have inherited a mild version of his father's illness—given, of course, his father was ill? My mind was in such a state of confusion by now, I didn't know just what to think.

Most of our conversation had been taken up by his trying to convince me that he was insane, which was certainly not the behavior of a normal man. On the other hand, nor was it the behavior of a mad one. No, the whole thing just didn't make sense.

According to all the books I'd read and the movies I'd seen, love was supposed to be a wonderful experience that sets bells ringing and nerve ends tingling in joyful anticipation of future warmth and happiness. So far, I thought despondently, mine had brought me nothing but heartache and misery. And yet, when I cast my mind back to the too-few carefree days Brett and I had spent together at the Abbot's House, I knew that it could be all the things it was supposed to be—if only there weren't this dreadful mystery separating us. Whatever happened, I knew how I would remember him—as a handsome knight-errant of the arts, leaning over the balustrade of his eagle's nest, regaling me with legends of olden times as the twilight darkened over his beloved Périgord. If only we could recapture those magical moments!

A bittersweet love, I thought wryly, running my hands over my shoulders, where I could still feel the bruising touch of his viselike grip.

"Of course," the doctor would say in his cold, logical way, "he grabbed you by the shoulders to act out his violence, to prove to you that he could be dangerous."

And in a way, I thought, the doctor would be right. It had, indeed, been an act to try to prove that very thing. But it hadn't been performed by a madman. On the contrary, it had been a deliberate and calculated move by a perfectly sane man, a man whom I loved with all my heart and who obviously needed my help. But . . . .

For the rest of that afternoon and into the early evening, I mulled the problem over in my mind. I got precisely nowhere. All I had were a number of facts that made no sense at all and a myriad of half-formed suspicions. None of those made any sense, either.

There was only one thing to do. I got into my little Renault and drove over to the Château Donazac. Quite apart from the fact that I needed a sounding board for some of my ideas, I badly needed to confide in someone I knew I could trust. Anne, Catherine and I had become firm friends over the past month or so, and I felt I could trust them with my life, if necessary. Then, too, some local support might not come amiss. I was, after all, a foreigner on my own, involved in matters that, in theory at least, were none of my business.

I found Anne on the terrace of the château. In the waning light of evening, she was working on some petit-point embroidery for the back of an antique chair.

"That's a lovely pattern," I said to break the ice. "Is it medieval? It looks perfect for the château."

"Fooled you," she said with a laugh. "It's Victorian and it's for my apartment in Paris." Noticing my drawn features, she frowned slightly and changed her tone. "You don't look well," she said worriedly. "Are you still having trouble with your sore throat?"

I sat down in one of the large, orange-covered armchairs, feeling very depressed. "It's not my cold that's bothering me," I sighed, "it's something quite a bit more serious than that."

Anne had stopped plying her needle, and now she looked at me closely. "If you want to take me into your confidence, don't be embarrassed," she said quietly. "I know how to keep secrets."

"Anne, you're the answer to a maiden's prayer," I replied sincerely. "I was feeling all alone in the world and I badly need a friend."

"Well, here I am."

Without pausing for comments, I told her the whole story. As she listened to me, her eyes reflected first amusement, then keen interest.

"I remember hearing something about the people at Delacour," she remarked when I'd finished. "Their unsociable character has been the subject of conversation around here for years. The old lady, while she was still alive, didn't have any friends to speak of and she lived alone with her young grandson. After her death, the older grandson came back to live on the estate, but he was no more outgoing than his grandmother. People said he didn't get along with his wife, but that may well be just a rumor.

"When he died a few months ago, there were all sorts of speculations floating around. There were several versions of how he died, but I think his death was finally classified as accidental. I have to admit that all this happened while we were away, and I only heard about it secondhand.

"The Abbot's House has been in ruins for years. That's why we were all so surprised when you told us you'd met someone living there. Was it really Brett Briançon? They say he escaped from Dr. Kloster's establishment and was hiding out there."

I nodded my head in agreement. With a force that surprised even me, I said, "I'm convinced that there's some underhanded scheming involved in this whole affair, and that Brett's bearing the brunt of it."

"Oh, come on now," Anne objected. "This sounds like something out of the late show! Surely you don't think he's being kept at Dr. Kloster's against his will. After all, Dr. Kloster himself would have to be involved, and I doubt that very much. I know him well, and I can assure you he's perfectly honest."

"Oh, I agree. The doctor is acting in good faith, I'm sure of that. And his hospital is not prison. He's positive Brett went there of his own free will, and I must say that that was confirmed by Brett himself. But Anne, none of it makes any sense. I'd like to wring that woman's neck!" I exclaimed angrily.

"What woman?" queried Anne, obviously surprised by my outburst.

"Alys Briançon." I spoke the name with all the assurance of my convictions. I wondered why, with each passing hour, I was becoming more and more certain that I was on the right track. I wondered if this certainty was a product of some slow process in my subconscious mind or had arisen from the gradual accumulation of gestures, words and acts that had awakened my suspicion little by little. All at once I knew for a fact that I'd stumbled onto a dreadful conspiracy.

"Dawn, what on earth are you talking about?" asked Anne completely bewildered. "What has Alys Briançon got to do with Brett's condition?"

"Everything!" I replied firmly. "I'm certain of it. Listen. . . ." And I went on to describe my first night in the Périgord, when Brett had tried to reenter his home and had nearly been caught. I told her about the lies I'd been fed by Alys and Charles, and all the other little things I'd learned that had struck a false note and made me suspicious.

"I must say, it doesn't make much sense," said Anne, slowly and thoughtfully. "Why would Brett return home that night when he must have known someone might be lying in wait for him? For that matter, why did he stay in the area at all if he wanted to escape? And, having escaped, why did he go back to the clinic so willingly when Alys discovered him at the Abbot's House?"

"You see," I interjected triumphantly. "You're beginning to think there's something wrong, too."

"Mmm, maybe," she conceded showly,

I sensed that she needed further convincing. "Why would Alys and Charles lie to me unless they had something to hide?" I pointed out. "Why tell me Brett was in love with his sister-in-law unless they hoped it would make me lose interest in Brett? They seemed awfully pleased with themselves when they thought they'd convinced me to leave the area."

"You have a point there," agreed Anne, after a moment's reflection.

Placing my hand on her wrist, I looked her in the

eyes. I sincerely hoped that she could read in mine my desperate plea for help. "Anne," I said, "I'm a foreigner. I can't do anything by myself; nobody will listen to me. But you can help me. Please help me to rescue Brett from this infernal trap."

Her intelligent face was moved to compassion. "Dawn, do you realize what you're asking me to do?" she said gently. "You want me to help you remove a patient from a private clinic, in spite of the fact that the patient told you himself that he went there of his own free will. What an absurdity, my poor dear!"

"I know, I know," I said. "I'm the one who seems insane with my suspicions. And yet, I'm sure that Brett isn't crazy. I'm absolutely positive. Please help me, Anne."

She thought about it for a moment, her fingers pressed against her forehead. Distractedly, I watched her lovely auburn hair as it billowed slightly in the breeze. Finally she stood up and collected her wool and her embroidery frame.

"I have an idea," she said. "Let's go and present your case to Bertrand. He'll tell us we're both crazy; but, perhaps, after he's thought about it for a while, he'll think of something that we missed. He's very down-to-earth and clearheaded. After all, he's a criminal lawyer; mysteries of this sort are his business. And even if he can't solve it for us, he can at least advise us on any legal aspects.

"Bertrand has always been a champion of lost causes," she continued, as she led me down the hall to her brother's study. "Once he gets stirred up over a situation, he can do the impossible. I've seen it many times. I guess that's why he became a lawyer in the first place.

"If he believes you—and if he's in the mood to help out a damsel in distress—he'll move heaven and earth to see that justice is done. He has three weeks' vacation coming up and he hasn't said anything about going away. As long as he's not planning to fly off to Tunisia or somewhere, we have a good chance of getting him to help us."

As luck would have it, the globe-trotting Bertrand had decided, for once, to spend his summer vacation at the château. And, as he had no special projects, he took an enthusiastic interest in my cause.

Between us, Anne and I filled him in on the story and all my suspicions. For a moment after we'd finished, he remained silent and thoughtful, a strange gleam in his eye. "So," he murmured finally, "Charles Courtney is playing prince consort to Alys Briançon, is he?"

"You know Charles?" I asked in surprise.

"Not personally," he admitted, "but I certainly know of him. I don't suppose there's a lawyer in Paris who doesn't."

"Is he really so famous?" I murmured, finding it hard to believe that the pompous and patronizing Charles Courtney could be well thought of by anyone, much less his peers.

"Perhaps 'infamous' would be a more apt description," replied Bertrand with a grin. "Don't get me wrong," he continued quickly as he saw a look of hope on my face. "There's no doubt he's a brilliant courtroom lawyer. But, for all that, there's something fishy about his business—a few too many obvious criminals going scot-free, that sort of thing. Nothing we can pin on him, of course, or we'd have had him disbarred years ago, but everyone suspects he's not quite to be trusted."

"And you think his presence in this instance indicates that something 'fishy' might be going on?" asked his sister.

"It might," agreed Bertrand. "It's certainly worth looking into. You know," he added. "I'd love to put that man behind bars. I dislike crooked people intensely, and a crooked lawyer's the worst."

"Of course," he went on more briskly, "this isn't going to be easy. It's a pity we don't know more about the family in general. In my years of practice, I've often found that many cases can be solved simply by knowing the background of the people concerned.

"For example, it might help us to know something about the relationship between Alys and Maurice before we worry about the one that may or may not exist between Brett and Alys. Rumor around here has it that they didn't get along very well, but we don't know that for sure, do we?"

"But doesn't the fact that Brett inherited the estate rather than Alys indicate that husband and wife weren't getting along very well?" queried Anne.

"Not necessarily," replied Bertrand. "Estates can be tied up in the most confusing ways, you know."

"Norman!" I exclaimed suddenly, sitting bolt upright in my chair. Noticing the startled looks on the faces of my two companions, I hastened to explain. "Norman's my brother," I said. "In fact, it's all his fault that I've got myself involved in the wretched mess." I went on to explain the relationship between my brother and Maurice. "I'm sure Norman will be able to tell us a lot about the family," I added, then glanced at my watch. "It's eleven o'clock now. Montreal's six hours behind us, which means that with any luck he'll just be getting home from work. You have a phone at the château, don't you?"

"Yes, and by all means use it," replied Bertrand, jumping to his feet. He looked as eager as I felt. "The sooner we start our inquiries, the sooner we can put Charles where he belongs."

He led me to the phone, and I quickly dialed the overseas operator.

Chapter 16

It seemed to take forever. In a fever of impatience I waited for an end to all the clicks and buzzes involved in connecting two telephones separated by some three thousand miles of North Atlantic Ocean. "Please be home, Norman," I whispered. "Please be home."

At long last, I heard a ring at the other end of the line, a click, then to my great relief, a familiar voice. "Hello?"

"Norman!" I exclaimed excitedly. "Thank God you're home!"

"Who is this?" came my brother's puzzled voice.

"Well, that's encouraging, I must say," I replied teasingly. "Do you mean to say that I've been gone so long you've forgotten my voice already?"

"Dawn? My God, it is you! But where are you calling from? Not France, surely?

"Yes, from France."

"Good heavens! Well, you're lucky you caught me in. I've only just got back from the office."

"I figured as much. That's why I called now. But listen, Norman, can we dispense with the pleasantries for now? I badly need your help, and it's going take long enough to explain everything to you as it is. I'm using the phone of some friends of mine and this call is going to cost an arm and a leg. I don't want to prolong it any longer than necessary."

"Of course. I'll help you in any way I can, little sister," replied Norman promptly, though I detected a note of surprise in his voice. "What's the problem?"

"Well, it's all got to do with your friend Maurice," I began, and for the third time that evening I ran through the story.

Norman, bless his heart, heard me through without interruption. "Well," he said, when I'd finished, "you certainly seem to have got yourself into the devil of a mess. But I don't really see how I can help you."

"When you first asked me to check up on Maurice for you, you mentioned he'd written to you in connection with a problem on which he'd wanted your help and advice. Did that problem have anything to do with his wife?"

There was a dead silence on the other end of the line. "Norman?" I queried anxiously after a moment.

"I'm still here," he said. "But look, Dawn, Maurice wrote to me in confidence, and I really don't think—"

"For goodness sake, Norman," I interrupted irritably. "Your loyalty to an old friend is touching, truly it is, but Maurice is dead now and nothing can hurt him anymore." It was callous of me, I knew, but my brother could be very exasperating at times, and this was one of them. "Brett is still very much alive and appears to be in big trouble. So, please, tell me everything you know."

"Oh, very well," sighed Norman. "Yes, Maurice's problem had to do with his wife."

"The story around here is that they didn't get along. Is that true?"

"Not exactly. As far as I could make out, Maurice was still very much in love with Alys, but she was rapidly tiring of him. He mentioned something about too many wild parties with old flames—that sort of thing. I rather got the impression that he wanted to get her out of Paris and was thinking of coming to Canada. But he wanted to discuss job opportunities with me first."

"And then when his grandmother died, he decided to settle at Delacour instead," I suggested. "He probably figured that it was far enough away from Paris to prevent Alys from attending wild parties."

"Something like that, I should think, yes," he agreed. "Look, little sister, I get the impression that Brett means, well . . . rather a lot to you. Am I right?"

"He means everything to me," I replied fervently.

"In that case I think I'd better let you in on another Briançon family secret. Maurice told me this one evening when he was feeling more depressed than usual. I remember it particularly because his father had just died and I was surprised he wasn't making plans to attend the funeral. When I asked him about it, he told me there wasn't any point since his father had been dead to him for many years, ever since he'd been diagnosed as incurably insane."

"I already knew he was insane," I interjected. "I also know he died in an asylum." Obviously Brett had told the truth on that score, at least.

"Don't interrupt," admonished my brother, adopting a severe tone. "I haven't finished yet."

Inwardly I sighed. My brother, I knew, could be surprisingly stubborn at times, and I could tell by the tone of his voice that this was one story he was going to tell in his own way, no matter what I said or how long it took. Mentally shuddering at the telephone bill we were racking up as the minutes ticked by, I settled myself back in my chair and prepared to listen to a long-winded version of Maurice's life. I only hoped it would be worth it.

"Understandably, I was a bit startled by this news," Norman continued, "but Maurice looked so bitter and gloomy, I invited him to take me into his confidence, which he willingly did.

"It seems that his father had been insane for many years, and had to make frequent and prolonged visits to mental hospitals for treatment. His family looked upon his illness as a blot on its honor and concealed the fact as carefully as they could. So they spread around the story that he had something to do with the diplomatic service and had to make frequent trips abroad. Only his family and closest friends knew that during his and his wife's absences from Delacour, he was, in fact, undergoing treatment in a mental hospital.

"Maurice's mother was still a young woman, and her life with her husband was a living hell. His mental condition turned him into a hard drinker subject to fits of violent temper. Understandably, after a while, she found this life unbearable. Circumstances prevented her from remarrying, but she could, and did, discreetly make a new life for herself—with one Roland Laurensac, who lived in—"

"Mexico," I breathed, visualizing in my mind's eye the imposing portrait hanging in the place of honor in the Delacour living room.

"You know about Laurensac?" asked Norman, surprised.

"Let's just say I've heard the name before," I replied hastily. "But never mind that now. Carry on with your story."

"Well, anyway, when people thought she was in far-off diplomatic posts with her husband, Mrs. Briançon was really in Mexico with Laurensac. Her husband's condition was so poor, both mentally and physically, that he wasn't expected to live long. I can only assume that she hoped one day to legalize her situation with Laurensac, because not long after she first stayed with him, she became pregnant."

"What!" I yelped, hardly able to believe my ears. "Are you trying to tell me that—"

"Brett and Maurice were only half-brothers," he finished for me placidly. "Yes, Brett wasn't Briançon's son, but Roland Laurensac's. So you can at least set your mind to rest on one score. Brett couldn't possibly have inherited any insanity from his father. Laurensac was a perfectly normal man."

"Was Brett ever told he wasn't Briançon's son?"

"That I don't know for sure. Certainly when Maurice told me the story, Brett was still under the impression that he was a Briançon. Whether Maurice or his grandmother ever told him the truth, I don't know."

"How about Alys?"

"Again, I can't really say for sure, although I suspect Maurice confided in her even before they were married. He wasn't the type to keep the family's skeleton a secret from someone he intended to live with for the rest of his life. He'd want to make sure of her feelings on the subject beforehand."

"Why didn't Mrs. Briançon ever marry Roland Laurensac after her husband died?" I asked. "At least, I assume she didn't marry him."

"No, she didn't, and that was what Maurice was so glum about the day he told me all this. In some ways, the saddest part about the whole story is that not two days before Mr. Briançon finally passed away, Laurensac became tired of waiting and married another woman."

"Well!" I exclaimed breathlessly, still finding it hard to believe what I'd just heard. "You've certainly dropped a bombshell, Norman. I'm not sure where it all fits in, yet, but thank you for telling me, anyway."

"Not at all," he replied warmly. "I only hope it will be of some help. Let me know, via the mails this time, how you get on, won't you?"

"I will," I promised. "Goodbye for now, Norman, and thanks again."

"Goodbye, little sister. Take care."

Dropping the receiver back on its hook, I tore down the hall to tell Anne and her brother what I'd learned.

"Well, you look mighty pleased with yourself," remarked Anne, as I burst unceremoniously into Bertrand's study. "Do I gather the phone call was a success?"

"I'll say," I replied excitedly. "Listen to this!" And I repeated everything Norman had told me.

"I wonder if Brett *does* know he's Laurensac's son?" mused Anne as I finished my tale. "If he does, then he's certainly faking his illness. But why?"

"That," I said determinedly, "is something I fully intend to find out tomorrow morning." I got to my feet. "Right now, it's getting late and I must leave you two in peace. I probably won't sleep a wink after all this excitement, but it isn't fair of me to keep you from your beauty rest as well."

As it happened, I was wrong. I slept like a log, and the sun was high in the sky when I woke the following morning. Scolding myself for being such a lazybones when there were important matters to attend to, I hurriedly got dressed and climbed into my car.

I took the by-now-familiar route to the clinic. As soon as I crossed the threshold of Dr. Kloster's private establishment, I detected a change in the atmosphere. The nurse at the reception desk, who'd been very friendly the day before, now called to me in an imperious voice, "Where are you going, miss?"

"To see Dr. Kloster," I murmured, taken aback. "I want his permission to see one of his patients."

"Your name, please?"

I was astonished. Yesterday they hadn't made such a fuss. I gave her my name and occupation.

"And whom do you want to see?"

"Mr. Brett Briançon."

She raised her eyes from the clipboard on which she'd

been recording these details. With an abrupt gesture, she thrust it aside. "I'm afraid that's impossible," she said firmly. "Mr. Briançon isn't allowed any visitors right now."

I raised an eyebrow questioningly. "Oh? And why not, might I ask? I didn't have any trouble getting permission to see him yesterday."

"We received special instructions early today, from the family and Dr. Kloster. No visitors."

"Has something happened to Mr. Briançon?" I asked, rather nervously.

She shook her head. "I can't tell you anything, miss."

"In that case," I replied, "I'll just have to ask Dr. Kloster."

"The doctor's not in."

"Ah! I see," I said coldly. For a moment there was silence while I chewed on my lip, deep in thought. Finally I asked, "Do your 'special instructions' include anything about Mr. Briançon's mail?"

"N-no."

"In which case, a letter could be delivered to him, right?"

"I,er, I suppose so," agreed the nurse hesitantly.

"Good." Fumbling in my purse, I found a pen, tore a sheet of paper from my notebook, and after a few moments' reflection, scribbled a short note.

Have made some startling discoveries. Donazacs also working on your behalf. Don't worry, we'll have you out of here in no time. Sorry about note, but you-know-who has forbidden me to see you. Am going to have showdown with her today.

With a flourish I signed it and, borrowing an envelope from the clinic, placed it inside and sealed it pointedly in front of the nurse.

"Please see that Mr. Briançon gets this as soon as

possible," I commanded imperiously. Then I turned and stalked out of the hospital.

I was seething with anger. Alys was obviously keeping a close watch on her prisoner and orders had been given. If I'd needed any further evidence that Brett was the victim of some vicious, underhanded conspiracy, that was it.

My poor little car suffered badly on the way over to the Donazacs. In my fury at Alys's connivings, I flung it around corners and ground gears viciously, so that by the time I pulled in front of the château, there was a decidedly unpleasant smell coming from the engine. *Too bad*, I thought maliciously, as I climbed out of the car and strode off in search of Bertrand.

It was midafternoon by now, and I fully intended to confront Alys that day. But Bertrand had promised to start his investigations first thing that morning, and I wanted to know what, if anything, he had turned up. I knew I'd need every bit of information I could lay my hands on if I was to induce Alys to show her hand.

Bertrand looked up from his desk with a smile when I entered his study. "I think out little investigation has opened up rather a large can of worms," he said cheerfully, "although, I must admit, I'm still not sure where it all leads."

"We can figure that out later," I replied, sitting down in one of the leather armchairs. "Right now, I'm dying of suspense. What have you found out?"

"Well, for a start, I've learned that Maurice didn't actually die of a head injury, but of a heart attack. That was according to the pathology report at the hospital. Apparently he'd had a heart condition for years and his days were numbered, anyway. According to the medical reports, he only regained consciousness in the hospital long enough to see Alys once and to swear out an affidavit absolving Brett from any responsibility for his death. He claimed he'd had the heart attack while standing on a stepladder or something, and had struck his head in the resulting fall. The only thing I don't understand is where the rumor of a fight with his brother came from."

I do, I thought grimly, thinking of the visit I had to pay later that day. Dear Alys again! "But why did Maurice bother to swear out an affidavit, anyway?" I asked. "If he died of a heart attack, surely Brett wasn't responsible at all. In fact, it sounds as if Brett had nothing to do with his brother's death."

"There had been talk of a fight—word travels fast in an area like this, Dawn—and according to the lawyer who'd accepted Maurice's affidavit, Maurice was anxious that his brother not be held responsible for it. Apparently Alys was most anxious to have Brett arrested and charged with manslaughter at the very least, but Maurice refused. And in case he died, by filing the affidavit he ensured that Alys could take no action in the future."

"I don't understand," I said, rapidly becoming more and more confused. "How, then does Brett end up in a mental institution?"

"Yes, well," said Bertrand. "That's the bit I'm still working on." He then asked me about my own day so far.

My blood beginning to boil again at the memory, I recounted the event of my ill-fated trip to the clinic.

"Mmm, the whole thing really does seem a little odd," agreed Bertrand thoughtfully when I'd finished. "What bothers me even more, though, is the fact that Alys has somehow managed to persuade Brett to sign a power of attorney in her favor."

"What!"

"I thought that might startle you," he remarked mildly. "It gave me quite a shock, too, and I must admit it tends to make me believe that Brett really is insane: either that or she has some tremendous hold over him we know nothing about. In some ways, it would help if we know for sure whether, at the time of the inquest, she was aware of the fact that Brett's real father was Rolland Laurensac.

"Well, all I can do is try to get some answers out of her when I see her tonight."

"You're going to see Alys tonight?"

"I want to know why she won't let me see Brett."

"Do you think that's wise?" asked Bertrand, concern showing on his kindly face. "I doubt she'll tell you anything, and you may be setting yourself up for something you can't handle."

"I hardly think I'll be in any serious danger," I replied with a smile. "You never know, she may drop the odd hint or clue we can work on. At the moment, all we seem to be doing is going around in circles. Why would she want Brett to sign a power of attorney in her favor, anyway?"

"I really don't know," confessed Bertrand with a sigh. "I've been racking my brains over that one all day. The only thing I can come up with is that she wants control of Delacour Manor, which, by the way, was inherited by Brett under some complicated old family will that Maurice never bothered to have contested or changed. But I can't see why Alys would want it. After operating expenses are deducted, the estate can't provide much more than a meager living."

"Couldn't she sell it?"

"Yes, but I would imagine she'd have a hard time finding a buyer, considering the lack of modern conveniences."

"How about the furniture? There are quite a few valuable pieces there."

"Maybe," conceded Bertrand, "but I can't see that the amount she'd receive for them would warrant the lengths she *appears* to have gone to to obtain Brett's inheritance."

"'Curiouser and curiouser,'" I murmured, feeling not

unlike Lewis Carroll's Alice must have felt when she'd uttered the well-known phrase.

"Isn't it, though," Bertrand agreed. "But look, it's nearly dinnertime. It's no use us thrashing this around anymore this evening. Why don't you stay and have dinner with us and try to forget about it, at least for a couple of hours? Then you can trot off to visit Alys and we can get together again on it tomorrow morning."

It was, I decided after a moment of reflection, a wonderful idea.

IT WAS already getting dark when I turned the car onto the rutted driveway of Delacour Manor. As usual, the place looked deserted, and somehow rather menacing as the nighttime shadows crept over it.

Undaunted, I climbed from the car and walked resolutely to the front door. Lucy took her time to answer my imperious summons, and when she did finally appear, it was to inform me that her mistress was out for the evening.

"In that case," I declared firmly, "I'll simply have to come in and wait for her." And so saying, I stepped over the threshold before Lucy had a chance to protest. I was quite determined to see Alys, come hell or high water, and I didn't care if I had to wait all night.

"Well, if you insist," grumbled the old servant. "But you'll be left on your own. I've got things to do and then I'm going to bed."

"No problem," I told her cheerfully. "I'll just sit quietly and read a magazine or something till she arrives. I won't bother you."

True to her word, Lucy led me reluctantly to the living room, then disappeared.

Left to my own devices, I sat down and began to leaf through one of the many magazines piled on a side table near the fireplace. But I really wasn't concentrating on what I was reading, and pretty soon my mind began to wander. I had the distinctly uncomfortable feeling that someone was spying on me, and looking up, saw the portrait of Roland Laurensac glaring down at me from it's place of honor above the fireplace.

Little do you know what trouble you've caused, I thought wryly. I suddenly realized that I'd forgotten to ask Bertrand if he'd managed to find out anything about Brett's real father. But then, I was sure he would have told me if he had.

My eyes wandered around the rest of the room, seeing once more the fine pieces of furniture that had so impressed me on my first visit. But, beautiful though they were, I had to admit that Bertrand was probably right. They weren't worth all the intrigue Alys seemed to be up to.

Night had fallen completely by now. I was becoming increasingly restless and began to pace back and forth. The sounds of the night insects echoed loudly in my ears, and one sudden sound made me jump. My lonely vigil for the one woman who I was sure could answer all my questions was beginning to tell on my nerves.

Aimlessly I wandered over to one of the windows, but all that greeted me as I looked out was unending inky blackness. *No moon to light the way tonight*, I thought. I recalled, with an involuntary shudder, the panic I'd felt that night when I'd thought some prowler had been trying to break in. And, after all that, it had proved to be Brett.

What a pity I hadn't known that at the time, I thought. Perhaps I could have helped him then and we wouldn't have had to go through all this anguish. Why had he come that night, I wondered. What had he been looking for?

Gradually, as I continued to stare unseeingly out of the window, an idea began to take root in my mind.

Lucy had probably gone to bed long since, and I was alone in the main part of the house. Why didn't I try to find it for him?

Of course, I had no idea what I would be looking for, but given all the events of the preceding month, it was reasonable to suppose that it was a legal document of some sort. I almost gave up on the idea right then and there, because any such document would obviously be locked up in a safe. And even if I were lucky enough to find a safe in this vast house, I certainly wouldn't have been able to open it.

But supposing it were a document Alys wanted no other member of the household to see? Surely the safest place to hide it would be in her own bedroom. Well, it was worth a try, anyway.

Remembering that most of the upstairs had no lights, I got a candle from the drawer where I remembered Alys kept them. I lighted it, then walked out of the living room into the hallway. The flickering flame sent weird shadows dancing across the walls. In the deathly silence that filled the isolated old mansion buried deep within the forest, they looked for all the world like some macabre beings performing some ghastly, unearthly ritual.

They followed me as I crept up the stairs, fearful that Alys might return at any moment. Opening the door of the room I knew to be hers, I stepped inside, and sweeping the candle around in a wide arc in front of me, looked around. It was furnished comfortably, but severely, with no hint of femininity whatsoever, and I was rather taken aback at its cold and impersonal starkness.

I cast the candle around once more and in its dim light caught sight of a black leather box sitting on top of the dresser. As I drew closer, I saw it had a small gold lock on the front. *Probably a jewelry case,* I thought, putting the candle down on the dresser. *I hope to God it's not locked.*

It wasn't, and I opened it, slowly, hesitantly, almost afraid of what I might find. But, as I peered inside and saw the buff envelope lying on the velvet in solitary splendor, I knew I'd struck pay dirt. For its was addressed to "Mr. Brett Briançon," and bore a Mexican stamp.

My heart was pounding now, as with trembling fingers I picked up the envelope and withdrew the sheet of heavy linen notepaper inside. Moving closer to the candle, I unfolded it and began to read.

It was from a legal firm in Mexico. "With regret," it informed Mr. Brett Briançon of the death of Roland Laurensac, who had been one of its most valued clients for many years. It was thus its duty to act as executor to his estate, not a difficult job, it appeared, since Laurensac had named Brett as his sole heir.

As I gazed in disbelief at the, to my mind astronomical, figure Roland Laurensac had been worth at the time of his death, my eyes widened in sudden, startling comprehension. "So this is what it's all about!" I whispered.

And then I froze in panic. "Looking for something?" inquired an icy voice from behind me. "Perhaps I can help."

I whirled, and to my horror saw not only Alys, but also Charles, standing on the threshold of the room. Her green eyes glittered cruelly in her waxlike face, and the expression of positive evil twisting her perfect features sent a cold shiver of fear down my spine. For his part, Charles looked completely calm and relaxed, and it wasn't hard to see why.

Glinting dully in the candlelight, and held in a remarkably steady right hand, was a particularly vicious-looking, snub-nosed revolver. And it was pointed straight at me.

Chapter 17

For an eternal instant in time, all three of us stood as though frozen. Gripped by sheer, unadulterated terror, I could only stand and stare in fascinated horror at the weapon in Charles's hand.

Alys was the first to break the spell of this motionless tableau. Stepping into the room, she walked toward me, her hand outstretched. "I think I'll take that, if you don't mind," she said.

Wordlessly I handed over the letter, wondering if I'd ever get the chance to tell Brett its contents.

"Well," said Charles cheerfully, "I think it's time we all adjourned to the living room for a little chat, don't you? Miss Charbonneau, if you'd be kind enough to lead the way. . . ."

I flinched as he casually waved the revolver in the general direction of the staircase. Realizing it would probably be folly in the extreme to disobey, I walked slowly out of the room and down the stairs, Alys and Charles close behind.

Once in the drawing room, I finally found my voice, although, understandably, it was somewhat tremulous. "What . . . are you going to do with me?" I whispered.

"That, my dear, rather depends on you," replied Charles, in the same cheerful tone he'd used before. "Do sit down, won't you? Can I get you something to drink?"

I shook my head, hardly able to believe my ears. To hear him talk, one would think we were all set for a pleasant evening's chitchat rather than a one-sided discussion on whether or not I should be allowed to live to a ripe old age. In fact, I had the rather unpleasant impression that he was thoroughly enjoying himself.

Having poured both himself and Alys a whiskey, he settled himself comfortably in an armchair and looked up at me, a smile on his florid face. "Well now, young lady," he said in a pleasant tone that didn't fool me for a minute, "your insistence on poking your nose into other people's affairs has got you into a spot of trouble, hasn't it?"

Is he asking me, or telling me, I wondered, remaining stubbornly silent. My question, I decided, was entirely academic. Either way Charles was right: I was in trouble—deep trouble.

"Why didn't you take the chance we offered you and leave when you could?" asked Alys suddenly.

"Because I didn't want to," I replied shortly. My initial fear was subsiding now, and was rapidly being replaced by a cold, unreasoning anger against these two poor excuses for human beings who'd cold-bloodedly plotted to deprive Brett of his inheritance.

"Nasty little thing, isn't she?" remarked Charles casually. "Now listen, young lady—" his voice suddenly became hard and ugly "—you have discovered a rather damaging piece of evidence that, understandably, we'd rather keep to ourselves. As you no doubt noticed, the sum mentioned in that letter is not inconsiderable, and I'm sure my client here—" with a nonchalant wave of his gun in Alys's direction "—would be quite willing to part with, say, one percent of it. In return for certain considerations, of course."

"Are you trying to buy my silence?" I demanded.

"Let's just say we're prepared to pay you for services

rendered, shall we?" replied Charles, a complacent expression on his face.

An instant later, it changed into one of disbelief as I burst into laughter. "You must be joking!" I spluttered. "Do you honestly think for one moment that I'm going to sit back and watch you destroy a man's life? Oh, no—"

I stopped abruptly as the revolver, which I'd actually managed to forget for a minute, was once more pointed in my direction. "Careful," warned Charles, a dangerous edge to his voice. "This isn't a toy, you know. I'd strongly advise you to reconsider your answer. You're not exactly in a bargaining position."

"Nothing doing," I replied flatly. After all, he wouldn't really dare shoot me—would he?

"Oh, dear," sighed Charles, getting to his feet. "I was rather afraid it might come to this. Your loyalty is most touching, my dear, but sadly misplaced, I'm afraid. Briançon is, after all, insane."

"Rubbish!" I retorted, still recklessly confident that Charles had no intention of really harming me. "I don't know what you and that . . . that *woman* over there have on Brett, but one thing I *do* know. Brett is no more insane than I am."

"How can you say such a thing!" exclaimed Alys. "He did kill a man, you know. His own brother, to be exact."

"And that's another thing I don't believe," I returned swiftly. "Brett may have a violent temper, but he certainly wouldn't have lost it over *you!*" To my great satisfaction, I heard Alys's sharp, hissing intake of breath as my barb shot home.

"And don't try to fob me off with stories about his father being insane," I added aggressively, feeling rather pleased with myself. "I know all about Roland Laurensac, too."

My complacency was very short-lived. In fact it vanished completely as Charles, his eyes no more than narrow slits, took a menacing step forward and I realized I'd gone too far. This was no friendly parlor game we were playing. It was deadly serious, and the stakes were high—Roland Laurensac's fortune and my life. And, as I looked at the gun in Charles's hand, I knew he held all the aces.

"Quite the little detective, aren't you?" he sneered nastily. "I think we've heard enough for one evening. Don't you agree, Alys?"

"Oh, quite," she replied airily. "More than enough. I think it's high time we taught her some manners. You can't really blame us, my dear. After all, it really wasn't very polite of you to snoop around my house in my absence."

"You're mad!" I gasped in horror, glancing feverishly around the room, desperately looking for something that could help me out of my predicament. I stepped hastily backward as Charles took another couple of paces toward me. "You're both stark raving mad! You'll never get away with it!"

"Oh, I don't know," replied Charles mockingly. "Accidents do happen, you know. Such a shame you had to visit the Abbot's House one last time. And it's positively criminal the way they let those tower stairs go to ruin. Someone could get badly hurt. I think one little shove ought to do it, don't you, Alys?"

Alys's answer was a peal of high-pitched mocking laughter and my blood froze in my veins. Moving surprisingly swiftly for a man of his size, Charles covered the short distance that separated us and grabbed me before I had a chance to react. His fingers bit cruelly into the soft flesh of my upper arm. "Come along, my dear. Time for us to leave."

"No!" I cried, and with a wrench that threatened to

separate my shoulderm I tore away from his viselike grip.

Dropping the gun, he came after me with both hands free.

"Let me go!" I screamed, struggling frantically to free myself from his powerful grasp. With a strength born of sheer desperation, I fought like a wildcat, using every bit of weaponry at my disposal—fingernails, fists, teeth and feet. Ignoring the sharp pains in my chest as my lungs cried out for oxygen, I kept pummeling away at him. I heard a muttered oath as I raked my nails across his face, and a grunt of pain as I sank my teeth into his forearm.

All at once, a blinding flash of light and pain exploded in my head. Then everything went black.

MY HEAD throbbed badly, but other than that I felt quite comfortable. Death wasn't so bad after all, I thought, pleasantly surprised, but it was awfully dark. And then I opened my eyes and discovered it wasn't dark at all. In fact, although blurred, it was startlingly, dazzlingly, white. I gave a soft moan of pain as the unexpected light hit my pupils and exploded in my already fragile head.

There was a rustle from somewhere nearby, then a shadow fell across my face. As I squinted up at it, my eyes gradually accommodated themselves enough to enable me to recognize it as a young woman, dressed in a crisp white uniform.

"Where am I?" I whispered.

"In the hospital," she replied in a low tone. "You've got a nasty crack on the head, but other than that the doctor says you're fine."

Concentrating hard, so as not to move any more than absolutely necessary, I reached up and carefully touched the bandage around my head. How had I managed to be so careless as to get myself into this state, I wondered. And then I remembered. With an involuntary shudder I closed my eyes in an attempt to block out the un-welcome memory.

After a few moments, I opened them again and asked, "How did I get here?"

The nurse gave me a warm smile. "I think I'll let your visitor tell you that," she replied, "as soon as you've taken these two tablets."

I winced as she helped me raise my head slightly and take the two white pills she proffered. Then I sank wearily back on my pillow and closed my eyes.

I heard the door open, then a low murmuring of voices. I caught the last two sentences spoken by the nurse before she left the room. "Not too long, now," she warned. "She's just had a sedative and the doctor wants her to get as much rest as possible."

Someone tiptoed across the room to the bedside. "Dawn?" came a hesitant voice. And it was the sweetest sound my ears had ever heard.

My eyes flew open and my heart gave a great lurch as I saw the handsome face of the man I loved staring anxiously down at me.

"Brett!" I whispered happily.

"Hi, Goldilocks," he said softly. "How do you feel?"

"I'll survive," I murmured with a weak smile. "But how did you—we—get here?"

"Are you sure you're up to hearing about it right now?"

I nodded, very slightly, but the movement was more than enough to send a sharp pain shooting through my head.

"Well, it was a good thing you left me that note. I hate to think where you might be now if you hadn't."

In a crumpled heap at the bottom of a crumbling stone staircase, I thought grimly, but remained silent as Brett continued his story.

"Unfortunately, it wasn't delivered to me until later

that evening," he went on, "and I was terrified that you would have already gone to see Alys. But I left Kloster's place, anyway, and went straight to the Donazacs. I'd suspected that Alys might not be alone for your little tête-à-tête and thought reinforcements might come in handy. As it happened I was right. I'm not sure where we'd be now if I hadn't had Bertrand's help.

"It didn't take long to persuade him that you might need help, either. I gather he'd already expressed concern at the idea of your visit to Delacour. Anyway, we burst into the house just in time to see Alys crack you over the head with the barrel of a particularly nasty-looking gun. And so . . . here you are."

"Thank you," I whispered. Then, remembering what he'd threatened after the last time he'd saved my life, I managed a weak grin and said, "It's a good thing they didn't try to drown me. I might be six feet under by now."

"Oh, I think I might have had a change of heart," he replied softly.

"Oh, Brett, I've got so many questions!"

"Later, my friend. They'll keep until after you've had a good long sleep."

I began to protest, but he cut me short. "No," he said firmly. "That sedative will start to work any moment now, and I have no intention of being insulted by my audience falling asleep in the middle of my narrative. I'll be here when you wake up, I promise."

I smiled up at him lovingly. Bending over, he planted a feathery-light kiss on my lips, then turned and left the room.

FEELING CONSIDERABLY more alive and aware of my surroundings after fourteen hours of uninterrupted sleep, I waited in a fever of impatience for the nurse to fetch my visitor.

It seemed like ages before Brett finally strode into the room. "So, the Sleeping Beauty has awakened at last," he remarked cheerfully, "without the help of a handsome prince, I hope."

I laughed. "Oh, Brett, it's so good to see you!"

"Delighted to be able to oblige," he replied in the casual manner I had come to know and love so well. Ignoring the chair set out by the nurse, he came and settled himself down on the bed, staring at me thoughtfully. "I must say, you're looking a little more like Dawn Charbonneau and less like the phantom of the abbey than when I saw you last," he declared, "but how do you feel?"

"Much better," I assured him. "The doctor says I can leave tomorrow."

"Thank God for that!" he murmured softly. "You really had me quite worried, you know."

"Mmm, it's a good thing I've got a hard head," I remarked, touched by his obvious concern.

"It's an absolute necessity around Alys, believe me," he replied darkly.

I sat up a little straighter against my pillows. "Speaking of Alys . . . ."

"I know, I know," he laughed. "You're dying of curiosity, right?"

"That's putting it mildly."

"Well, I'd hate to see the good doctor's ministrations go to waste. Where would you like me to start?"

"At the beginning of course."

Brett sighed. "Trust you to ask the impossible," he teased. Then he frowned slightly, and his voice took on a more serious note. "I suppose the whole thing really started when Maurice decided to settle down at Delacour. Alys wasn't too thrilled about the idea, to say the least—no more wild parties, no more theater nights and balls and no more secret and not so secret admirers, either. I'll never understand why Maurice didn't divorce the woman, but no matter what she did, he always stuck to her. He worshipped the ground she walked on!

"I suppose it was all my fault in a way. I'd been in Périgueux that afternoon—one of my occasional jaunts to get art supplies—and I happened to see Alys cheerfully walking down the main street arm in arm with another man. Stupidly, in the drawing room after dinner that evening, I made some passing reference to the effect that I hoped she'd enjoyed her little assignation. Words were exchanged, the conversation became heated, and before I knew what was happening Maurice marched over and landed a beautiful right uppercut square on my jaw."

"*He* attacked *you*?"

"Mmm, and I must say, he'd lost none of his old boxing skill," replied Brett feelingly. "My jaw ached for days. Anyway, he came at me again and I put out my arm to fend him off. For no apparent reason, he suddenly staggered, then dropped like a stone. Presumably that's when his heart gave out, but I didn't know that at the time. He must have struck his head hard on something on the way down, because he certainly had a head injury when he was admitted to the hospital, but I never saw exactly what happened."

"Hold it," I interjected. "What do you mean, you 'never saw exactly what happened'?"

He grinned. "I told you a hard head was a necessity around Alys, didn't I? She wields a poker as effectively as she does the barrel of a gun, believe me. She gave me an almighty crack on the head with the one in the drawing room."

My eyes widened in astonishment. "Why on earth did she do that?" I exclaimed.

"It's hard to say for sure. Possibly she saw it as a way to kill two birds with one stone—literally, although it was a poker in my case. She knew about Maurice's bad heart, of course, and perhaps had guessed that he'd had an attack and probably wouldn't live. With me out of the way, as well, and as my only living relative, she stood to inherit a great deal of money she'd be completely free to spend as she liked. With Maurice dead and me still alive, she had nothing. She knew Maurice had left the estate and all his money to me.

"Unfortunately for her, I also have a hard head and disobligingly refused to die. So she had to put plan two into effect and came to me with two choices. Either I could voluntarily submit to treatment for a mental condition, in which case I was also to sign a power of attorney in her favor, since I was incompetent to handle my own affairs. Or she would swear I had started the fight with Maurice and be charged with first-degree murder. Under the circumstances, I chose the former."

Slowly, I shook my head, wondering if I could possibly have heard right—and hoping I hadn't. Didn't he know about the affidavit? But then how could he? I was confused and rapidly becoming upset. I'd hoped for answers, and all I'd got so far were more mysteries.

"I don't understand," I murmured. "Neither of those choices makes any sense."

"I agree—now. At the time, it was a very different kettle of fish, I can assure you."

"But you didn't start the fight. In fact, you didn't fight at all," I objected. "You wouldn't have been charged with murder if you'd told the authorities what had happened. Why didn't you *defend* yourself?"

"I would have," replied Brett softly, "if I could have remembered what *had* happened."

There was dead silence between us as I digested this new piece of information. Then the light slowly dawned. "You mean—" I whispered.

"Exactly!" he broke in with a wry smile. "I'd lost my

memory. Oh, I knew who I was, where I was, everything about my background, that sort of thing. But I could not remember what had happened immediately before and during the fight. Retrograde amnesia, I think they call it. All I had was Alys's assurance that I had started it. Not that I believed her for one minute—I never did trust that woman—but I couldn't prove it. I couldn't tell anyone anything about it. I could hardly say 'Look, your honor, I know I didn't kill my brother, but I can't prove it. You'll just have to take my word for it,' could I? I don't think it would have got me very far."

"The court might have believed it if you'd explained that you'd lost your memory."

"*Might*," he pointed out. "Since I remembered everything else about myself so clearly, I considered it highly likely they'd think my sudden lapse of memory at that point in my life no more than a convenient excuse. Having no desire to spend the rest of my life behind bars, I opted for Alys's first choice. Then, too, she obviously had some underhanded scheme in the works and I wanted to know what is was. Under the circumstances, I felt my chances were a great deal better at Kloster's establishment than in prison. I knew my father—or who I'd thought was my father—had died in an insane asylum, and given my sister-in-law's tremendous talents as an actress, was quite sure she could carry the whole thing off."

"Did you know about Laurensac then?"

Brett shook his head. "No. My memory still hadn't returned the night we scared each other half to death, and I'd left the clinic and gone to Delacour in the hope that a return to the scene of the crime might trigger something on my mind. As you know, Charles's henchmen were lying in wait for me, as they were every night thereafter, when I tried over and over again to get back into the house. As you know, I managed to elude them that night, and the other times I went back. And during the day, I stayed in the Abbot's House. Courtney didn't think to look for me there, and Alys was away in Paris for nearly two months. When she returned, she knew exactly where to find me and hotfooted it over to the abbey to get me back to the clinic. She told me she'd found a psychiatrist in Paris who would agree to certify me if I didn't return there permanently. One of Courtney's shady connections, no doubt.

"That gave me a nasty shock, I must admit. I knew Alys was quite capable of having me locked away forever. I thought it was because she wanted the estate and the money—Maurice left quite a bit, in fact.

"I had consistently refused to give her power of attorney, though," Brett continued, "but she bided her time, assuring me nastily that my time in the clinic would eventually wear me down and I'd finally give in.

"In fact, by the time you arrived there that day, I really was beginning to feel a little sorry for myself. I didn't think I'd ever get out of the place, and was sure that if I had to stay there much longer I really would go crazy! Then I saw Alys cracking you over the head with a gun and the whole thing came back in a blinding flash."

"So you never knew that Laurensac was your real father?" I asked.

"I had no idea, Dawn. The first I knew of that was seeing the letter on the living-room table at Delacour when I came after you just the other night." Brett scratched his head in amazement. "So it wasn't just Maurice's money she wanted. She wanted me permanently locked away so she could get her hands on Laurensac's money, as well. Apparently—according to the postmark—that letter arrived a day or two before you arrived. That's why she took off so suddenly, I guess. She probably discussed the letter with Courtney, and the two of them decided on the idea of getting hold of that crooked psychiatrist who would agree to certify me—no doubt for a percentage of the take, as they say. A very clever scheme, really," Brett conceded with a smile. "I was taking just a little too long in handing her power of attorney.

"You were the only one who had any faith in me, Dawn," he said softly. "I was afraid you were getting in over your head and tried everything I could think of to persuade you to forget about me the day you came to the clinic. But no, you never lost faith or hope, and you very nearly got yourself killed. All because of me."

"Well, I could hardly sit back and watch them destroy your life and cheat you out of your inheritance, could I?" I protested, becoming a little flustered at the strange expression on his handsome face.

"I know," he said gently, "and one day that big heart of yours is going to get you into trouble again. I really think you need someone to protect you . . . my love."

As I gazed into those beautiful gray eyes, now filled with more love and tenderness than I'd have thought possible, an incredible feeling of hope spread slowly through me. "Is that . . . an . . . offer?" I whispered tremulously.

"It most certainly is!" he declared emphatically, and sweeping me into his arms, bandage and all, swept me away on a tide of passion and joy that promised to last forever.

And when, a little while later, the nurse came to check on her patient, she took one quick look into the room and then left, a soft smile of understanding on her face. After all, who was she to disturb the progress of love?